Peppermints

IN THE *Parlor*

BARBARA BROOKS WALLACE

Peppermints

IN THE *Parlor*

AN ALADDIN BOOK
Atheneum

Published by Atheneum
All rights reserved
Copyright © 1980 by Barbara Brooks Wallace
Published simultaneously in Canada by Collier Macmillan Canada Inc.
Manufactured by Fairfield Graphics
Fairfield, Pennsylvania
ISBN: 0-689-71048-8
First Aladdin Edition

Contents

1. Aunt Twice   *3*
2. Shadows in Sugar Hill Hall   *14*
3. Tilly   *23*
4. A Disturbing Explanation   *43*
5. Kipper   *53*
6. A Sad Arrival   *68*
7. Peppermint Peril   *82*
8. Fish Syrup   *89*
9. An Unexpected Invitation   *102*
10. Mrs. Poovey and Mrs. Loops   *113*
11. The Remembrance Room   *124*

12. A Midnight Visit   137
13. The Trapdoor   145
14. The Jolly Sailor   155
15. A Necklace of True Pearls   165
16. The Scary Indiwidual   171
17. A Stranger at Pa's Place   179
18. Peppermints in the Parlor   188

Peppermints
IN THE *Parlor*

For my niece
SUSAN SCHINDEHETTE
with love

ONE

Aunt Twice

The train rocking through the night gave a lonely wail. *Whoo! Whoo-whoo-whooey!* If ghosts had voices, that must be the way they would sound, Emily thought. Though settled in the comfort of a warm train compartment, she felt a sudden chill, and thrust her hands deeply into the white fur muff she held on her lap. Even her reflection in the window glass had a pale and unreal look, as if it were the ghost of a young girl outside the train trying to break in.

The flickering gaslight in the compartment appeared in the glass as a lantern, its light dancing eerily over the young ghost's head as she wandered the world to find a home. Shreds of fog, like pale fingers, brushed against the window. The train wailed again, and Emily could not help shuddering. What if *she* had to roam the world seeking a home, and never found one?

To reassure herself, Emily reached inside her green velveteen coat, pulled out the gold locket that hung from a chain around her neck, and opened the clasp. There, smiling back at her across from a small photograph of Mama and Papa, were Aunt and Uncle Twice, who were all the family she had left now.

It still puzzled Emily that she had not seen them in such a long time. She had asked questions about this, but had been told that Uncle Twice was occupied with business matters, or that Aunt Twice had gone off to New York for her new spring wardrobe. That was all that was ever said.

In any event, Mr. Dowling, Mama's and Papa's lawyer, had told Emily of Aunt Twice's letter, so Emily had no doubt that she and Uncle Twice would be there to greet the train when it arrived in San Francisco. Then once again Emily would be taken to the grand white mansion on the hill. She could still see it in her mind, even though she had only been a very young child the last time she was there.

Sugar Hill Hall! So named because Uncle Twice had bought the mansion with a fortune made in the sugar trade, it was grander even than Emily's own home had been. Now, somewhere in the distance, lights that could break through a fog as dark and thick as a witch's cloak

were twinkling for her, and that was what she intended
to think about. She would think only about the lights,
and the fire already crackling in the marble fireplace
that graced the huge, elegant parlor. She would think
only about—

Suddenly, the train lurched, and lurched again.
She clutched the red horsehair seat to keep from being
tumbled to the floor. Outside the windows, lights *were*
appearing. They were only the lights of the train station,
of course, but it meant the train had arrived at last.
The engine squealed in anguish as the brakes were
applied, belched forth clouds of angry steam, and finally
came to a groaning stop. Eagerly, Emily slid from her
seat and pressed her nose to the cold window to see if
she could catch a glimpse of beautiful Aunt Twice and
tall, handsome Uncle Twice, waving and smiling at her
to welcome her home!

§●

A deeper fog had begun to creep stealthily up from the
sea, spreading over San Francisco to dim the lights of
its buildings and turn them into monstrous shadows.
The fog wrapped itself silently around Emily as she
huddled with her travelling bag by the waiting room
door of the train station.

It was nearly an hour later, and no one had yet

come to greet her. Not Aunt Twice. Not Uncle Twice. Not anyone. Smudges of dirt from her long train ride already stained her white stockings and white, high-button shoes, but by now even the bright red ribbons knotted around her long golden braids had begun to droop. She shivered again and pulled her white fur tam-o'-shanter down about her ears, digging her chin deep into the collar of her velveteen coat. She had been trying to hold back the tears, but now they came perilously close to pouring down her cheeks.

Where were Aunt and Uncle Twice? Why had no one come to meet her? The streams of people passing by, deeply intent on their own cares and worries, looked through her as if she had indeed become a ghost. She stared at each face, hoping to find the one that would welcome her with a smile. But they all rushed past her, as if sucked up and swallowed by the fog. Would the fog eat her up too, she wondered, so that ever after she would be nothing but a ghostly face peering in train windows? The only reply she had to her question were two pinpricks of gaslight blinking murkily at her from across the street like rat's eyes. She turned from them with a shudder.

Then all at once she heard her name being called. "Emily? Emily Luccock?" It sounded dim and hollow as if mixed with a bowlful of the fog.

She looked around eagerly for a familiar face, but

all she saw was a strange woman approaching through the gloom. A shabby brown coat flapped wearily around her thin ankles. Her hair, of no particular color, straggled in drab, lifeless wisps from under a shapeless felt hat. Emily drew back, startled by the sight of the faded eyes set deep in the woman's face, the deathly pale lips, and the skin like parchment drawn tight over sharp cheekbones.

"Emily, my dear child, don't you know me? This is your Aunt Twice!"

Was it? Emily wondered with a sharp stab of fright. If so, where were the flyaway shining curls and dancing green eyes? Where was the fashionable coat with the nipped-in waist, and where the feathered Paris bonnet? And most important, where was the pink-cheeked face, as pretty as her own Mama's had been? How could this thin, sunken person be the Aunt Twice she had once known?

The strange woman hesitated, and finally smiled. With the smile, shadows of long-forgotten dimples came to her cheeks. A faint sparkle lit her eyes. She dropped to her knees and held out her arms.

"Aunt Twice!" Emily cried. She ran at last to bury her face in the worn woolen coat.

"My poor little girl!" Tears flowing down her cheeks, Aunt Twice held Emily away to look deeply into her face. "My poor, poor child."

Then all at once, Aunt Twice jerked sharply. With a sudden twist of her head, she turned toward the granite tower of the train station where a large, dimly lit clock peered through the fog like a pale, timekeeping moon. She stiffened and jumped to her feet.

"We must hurry, Emily! We must hurry! Is this the only travelling bag you've brought? Have you any trunks?" Fear made her voice sharp.

"T-t-two, Aunt Twice," Emily stammered. She was frightened once more by the sudden change in her aunt. It was as if Aunt Twice had turned into a stranger again. "Mrs. Leslie, Mama's and Papa's housekeeper, said they had been sent. Haven't they come yet?"

"No, but never mind. We must hurry now, Emily. Come along! We must not miss the next cablecar. We *can't!*" With no word of explanation, Aunt Twice snatched up Emily's bag and hurried across the sidewalk. Emily stumbled along beside her.

Her mind buried in her own troubled thoughts, Aunt Twice almost stepped off the curb in front of the horses of a tall black cab trotting to a stop in front of them.

"Cab, ma'am? It's a bad evening out." The heavy-jowled cabman spoke with the glum, disappointed air of having no hope for a fare.

But Aunt Twice looked over her shoulder once more at the station clock, and then opened her worn purse with trembling fingers. Lest she change her mind, the cabman wasted no time. Cape flying out, he leaped down, nimble as a frog, and flung open the cab door.

"Sugar Hill Hall on Pacific Street," Aunt Twice murmured to him in a voice barely above a whisper, and hurried Emily into the cab.

Tucked into a corner seat, Emily crossed her thin, white-stockinged legs neatly, and gave Aunt Twice a shy glance. Surely, Emily thought hopefully, now that the worry of getting home on time had been solved, she would be hugged once more and comforted for the terrible sudden loss of Mama and Papa in the boating accident at sea. And shouldn't she be given news of Uncle Twice? Why had he not come in his splendid red phaeton to fetch them at the station?

But Aunt Twice did not enfold Emily in her arms, and she explained nothing. Instead, she perched stiff and silent as a stone wall on the edge of her seat, moving her pale lips wordlessly from time to time. She appeared to have forgotten all about Emily.

Clop! Clop! Clop! Clop! The sound of the horses' hoofs drummed gloomily on the damp cobbled streets. Deep drifts of fog pressed against the windows, so she could see nothing but the dim flickering of an occasional lonely gaslight. Were they lost? She could not remember that Sugar Hill Hall was such a long ride from the train station. *Clop! Clop! Clop! Clop!* On and on they rode, horses' hoofs drumming outside, deadly silence inside, up one hill and down another. It seemed as if they had covered a dozen dark-filled miles before Aunt Twice turned suddenly and took Emily's hand in her own.

"Dear, darling child, will you promise me that no matter what happens, you will try to be a brave little girl, a *very* brave little girl?"

Be a brave little girl no matter what happens? What could that foreboding request mean? Emily was too frightened to do more than nod as she felt the chill of Aunt Twice's hand go through her like an icy needle.

The hand over hers tightened. Aunt Twice threw the cabman a furtive look and dropped her voice to a whisper. "Now there is something else you must promise me. When we enter the parlor of Sugar Hill Hall, you must let me give the replies to whatever questions are asked. Only speak if directly spoken to, and you must then agree with whatever I say. Be as polite as you know how. Please, darling Emily, will you promise all these things, for your sake and—for mine too?" Aunt Twice's voice broke in a hoarse sob.

Emily was more frightened than ever, and had only time to nod again when the cabman called out, "Sugar Hill Hall, ma'am!"

Aunt Twice gave a sharp gasp. "Please don't go into the driveway! Stop right here at once!"

The cab lurched to such a sudden stop that Emily was almost catapulted from her seat. She had no time even to peer out the window before Aunt Twice rushed

her from the cab. So it was not until her aunt was carefully counting out the coins from her worn purse and
placing them in the cabman's eager hand that she looked
up the broad driveway for her first glimpse of Sugar
Hill Hall. What she saw made her breath catch in her
throat. For unlike Aunt Twice, the great mansion was
exactly as Emily remembered it!

Through the fog and the deepening evening dusk
it loomed, seeming nearly four times the size of the
home she had left. Window after window reached endlessly across it, and the same giant columns held up the
lofty portico that greeted a wide, circular driveway.
But one thing she had forgotten was how brilliantly
white the mansion was. If the paint had grown shabby
like Aunt Twice, it was not noticeable in the dusky
mist. With its columns that looked like huge white
candy canes, the mansion did seem to have actually been
carved out of sugar!

Suddenly, Emily felt her heart leap. As the cab
lumbered off into the fog, and Aunt Twice clutched
her hand, half dragging her up the wide driveway, she
felt as if she wanted to laugh. And laugh and laugh!
Now at last she knew what this was all about. It was a
magnificent joke! Had Uncle Twice, long ago, not loved
to tease and surprise her with his jokes? And had Aunt
Twice not always encouraged him with her bubbling
laughter? If Sugar Hill Hall was still as grand and
beautiful as ever, how could anyone as sad and bedrag-

gled as Aunt Twice be living there? Emily had to choke back the laughter so she would not spoil Aunt and Uncle Twice's joke. For once inside that great door, she knew what she would find.

There would first, of course, be a joyous Uncle Twice with his arms outstretched to receive her. Behind him would be a welcoming fire popping and crackling in the marble fireplace. Lucy, the maid, would be standing beside it with a gleaming silver tray bearing fine white china cups, thin as eggshells, filled with steaming hot chocolate. Later, all smiles, she would pass crystal dishes heaped with little cream cakes, tiny sandwiches, and Emily's favorite strawberry tarts. With Aunt and Uncle Twice watching from the silk-covered settee, Emily would curl up on the thick, soft rug before the fireplace, tasting first one thing and then another as Aunt and Uncle marvelled at how her appetite had grown.

Finally, they would all go together to the room where Emily had once stayed, now redone all in white with pink rosebuds to match her own room at home. After they had shed tears over Mama's and Papa's photographs, Aunt and Uncle Twice would hug and kiss her, telling her how wonderful it was that she had come to live with them.

Even the strange darkness of the windows, as if no one could possibly be inside the mansion, did not fool

Emily. This was, she knew, Uncle Twice's very best joke!

They reached the steps to the portico, and Aunt Twice paused. "Promise me, Emily, with all your heart, that you will do the things I asked!" Her voice was stretched so tight and thin it was trembling.

"I promise, Aunt Twice!" Emily said happily. She could hardly keep from skipping up the steps.

She watched eagerly as Aunt Twice removed a large brass key from her purse and thrust it into the keyhole of the massive door. A moment later, the door swung open, and they stepped into Sugar Hill Hall. And into a dim, musty, cavernous parlor lit only by four small gas lamps flickering weakly on the walls, with no trace of any fire ever having been laid in the stone-cold fireplace. But Emily barely had time to notice this, because her eyes were instantly riveted to the two figures standing before them, and neither one was a laughing, rollicking, joking Uncle Twice.

Both were women, one plump as a pudding in a lavender, full-skirted dress. All Emily could see of her head, however, was a tiny lace doily set on a crown of greying hair. She kept her face bent over a pair of long knitting needles and was busily plying them as if she had no interest whatsoever in the new arrival. But it was the figure beside her that made Emily's blood suddenly freeze.

Click! Click! Click! To the curiously grim tune of the knitting needles, her eyes rose slowly up, up, up past the waist of a deadly black skirt, past a gold medallion with a glittering ruby eye in its center, past a high black collar coiled around a white, serpent-thin neck, past a chin sharp as an ice pick, past thin bloodless lips under a pale nose so pinched it seemed air could never pass through it, and arriving finally at the meanest, wickedest, evillest pair of eyes Emily had ever seen in her whole life!

TWO

Shadows in Sugar Hill Hall

The eyes stared at Emily, snake eyes that never moved, and yet she knew they were crawling over her inch by inch. She felt goose bumps of terror rising on her arms and legs.

Click! Click! Click! The needles knitted on, but the parlor beyond was silent, as her velveteen coat, white stockings, and fur hat were examined and measured, not to mention what was inside them. At least one whole row of stitches had clicked by before a verdict was delivered, from lips that barely took the trouble to move.

"She is puny for eleven, Mrs. Luccock!"

Aunt Twice drew in her breath sharply. Her knuckles showed white where she clutched her purse. "I—I don't understand, Mrs. Meeching. She was such a—a healthy, robust little child. Of course," she faltered, "it has been a long time since I've seen her. I—I had no idea . . ." Her voiced faded away.

By way of reply, Mrs. Meeching allowed a faint hiss of air to escape her nose.

Of course, the truth was that Emily had never been either healthy or robust. Born too early, which she knew from having overheard Mrs. Leslie whispering to someone once, she had always been frail and fragile as a baby sparrow. And she had always been tiny, so that even at eleven, she looked hardly more than eight. A long parade of physicians had poured bottles of potions and pills down her throat (most of which she had unfortunately poured right back up again), but none of them was able to bring the desired color to her cheeks, or add a quarter inch of extra fat to her thin legs. So although it had indeed been a long time since Aunt Twice had seen her, none of the rest was true. Aunt Twice, Emily knew, was lying. But now at last she understood the meaning of her aunt's dire warning, although it had hardly been necessary to give one. Emily could not have opened her mouth if her life hung on it. She stood staring at Mrs. Meeching with frozen round eyes, too scared even to tremble, like a small animal hypnotized by a cobra.

"She'll fatten up soon, I'm certain," Aunt Twice ventured palely, not sounding at all certain of anything. "Bearing in mind that the child has just suffered a terrible loss—"

A thin, interrupting eyebrow slithered up Mrs. Meeching's forehead. "We bear in mind what we choose to bear in mind, Mrs. Luccock. I pray, for her sake, as well as yours, that she *will* fatten up soon, but I warn you, it will not be at my expense. She will not be pampered either in the kitchen or at any dining table and will eat exactly what the others eat. Furthermore, she will earn her keep. That is clear, is it not, Mrs. Luccock?"

Although Mrs. Meeching addressed these grim orders to Aunt Twice, there was no doubt as to what person was intended to profit by hearing them. Her glance never flickered away from Emily for an instant.

"I suppose she is wearing a silk dress under that coat? Well, there will be no need for silks and velvets in scrubbing sinks, scouring pots, and emptying slop jars eh?" There was a brief pause to allow this to settle. "Has she other clothes, Mrs. Luccock?"

"Two trunks coming—" murmured Aunt Twice.

"Two?" The same thin eyebrow rose a trifle higher. "All filled with the same frivolous garments, I venture. Well, we'll have to attend to that, just as we shall have to attend to the hair. Long golden braids take entirely too much attention, wouldn't you say, Mrs. Luccock?"

If Aunt Twice agreed to this observation, it was hard to tell it from the small sound that escaped her throat.

"I collect," continued Mrs. Meeching smoothly, "that we might encounter some difficulty in having this matter attended to. Alas!" The *alas* came out sounding as far from what was originally intended for the word as anything imaginable. "Mrs. Plumly, the scissors, please!"

"Oh no!" breathed Aunt Twice. "Not her beautiful hair!"

"The scissors!" repeated Mrs. Meeching. Her eyes still fastened on Emily, she uncoiled a white, boneless hand in the direction of the plump lady with the knitting needles.

The knitting was arrested for a moment as Mrs. Plumly dipped into a capacious rose-embroidered knitting bag and handed Mrs. Meeching a pair of gleaming silver scissors, long as a dagger. With a flick of a pointed finger, Mrs. Meeching directed Emily to turn around. Then the scissors hissed open, and with a solid crunch, the silver jaws snapped together over one of her golden braids. *Hiss! Crunch! Snap!* went the scissors again, and she felt a sunny braid part from her head with a faint, farewell sigh and fall to the floor with a thump.

From the moment that Emily had walked through the doors of Sugar Hill Hall into its spectral parlor, she had half believed that she had stepped into a nightmare and would soon wake from it. But the sound and the feel of the silver jaws biting through her hair were all too real. Her heart was still pumping with fear, but with the loss of her braid, somewhere deep inside a large amount of terror was suddenly replaced by an equally large amount of anger.

How dared this wicked woman remove from her something she had owned most of her life and which had been so precious to Mama and Papa! One of her happiest memories would always be the one of skipping in to say good night to them in her pink nightdress. And how Papa had loved her hair, unplaited for the night, floating about her shoulders like a golden cloud! Now half of it was already lying lifelessly on the floor, and the rest soon to follow.

Why was Aunt Twice allowing this to happen? Why did she not put a stop to it at once? But when Emily looked at her aunt, she knew why. Though Aunt Twice's eyes were brimming with tears, her face was ashen with fear. So Emily stood still as a stone statue, without making a sound.

Thin as a thread, strong as wire! Papa had said that

once about her, she remembered, and everyone had laughed. But now she intended to prove Papa's words true. She would not cry and make a scene, for Aunt Twice's sake. This monstrous person wielding the scissors would not bring tears to *her* eyes.

Hiss! Crunch! Snap! Hiss! Crunch! Snap! A second braid lay beside the first, its bright red ribbon trembling like a butterfly on a dead branch. Emily dug her fingernails into her hand in a tight fist, but her eyes remained dry.

"There now, Mrs. Luccock, I believe she is ready to go to work. She will be expected to serve in the dining room this evening and to help Tilly so that you may be relieved for your other duties. And on the matter of dinner, I presume it will be served on time? You were very late returning, were you not, Mrs. Luccock?"

"I had to wait such a long time for the cablecar, you know, Mrs. Meeching. The fog must have held it up." Aunt Twice twisted her fingers together nervously.

"But I noticed that you *arrived* in a cab. Cabs are for the very rich." Mrs. Meeching's voice suddenly took on a sly quality. "We must be paying you too well, eh, Mrs. Luccock?"

"I didn't want to be late. It took all the money I had," said Aunt Twice faintly.

"Well, we shall see!" The scissors still in Mrs. Meeching's hand hissed open and snapped shut. "You may go now, and take the orphan brat with you."

Aunt Twice started to reach for Emily's travelling bag, but a warning hiss from Mrs. Meeching made her draw back her hand as if it had been bitten.

"There will be no pampering, Mrs. Luccock. Let her carry her own bag!"

Quickly, Emily wrapped both her small hands around the handle of her travelling bag and stumbled forward. To her dismay, she found that Mrs. Plumly stood directly in her path. She hesitated for a moment, and in that moment Mrs. Plumly finally looked up from her needles to present a round, blossom-pink face as harmless as an apple dumpling and to give Emily a secret, sympathetic smile. Emily nearly dropped her bag in surprise. Curiously, this unexpected friendliness from someone as warm and cozy as a story-book grandmother came close to making her cry at last. But under Mrs. Meeching's icy stare, she kept back the tears and steered around Mrs. Plumly as best and as rapidly as she could manage.

Now, for the first time, she could study the parlor that had once so delighted her. Although her bag thump-thumped painfully against her knees, she managed to peek upward. There they were, the same plaster cupids gamboling in the corners and all around the edges of the endlessly high ceiling. On either side, the walls were still graced with the same huge mirrors. And directly ahead the same broad oak staircase curved up to a high mirrored wall, and then up and up to a second and yet a third story. Emily remembered how she had loved to run up those stairs to her little room on the second floor. She hoped that Aunt Twice, if she could do nothing else, had arranged for Emily to have that very same room again.

Of course, everything she now saw in the parlor provided only a memory of an elegance long since past. The carpet under her feet was worn to the threads. The gold frames around the mirrors were tarnished and peeling. And cobwebs dangled like small ghosts from the cupids overhead. She could tell all this despite the shadows that shrouded the room.

Shadows seemed to be lurking everywhere. Shadows in the stairwell. Shadows hovering in the corners of the ceiling. Shadows even seemed to be huddling in every chair that lined the walls of the room. And then Emily made a horrifying discovery. In the dim, flickering light what had appeared to be shadows in the chairs were not shadows at all. They were very old people sitting and staring silently ahead with pale, wrinkled faces as empty of expression as unmarked gravestones!

Who were they? Why were they there? Had they been sitting in the room all along, watching the terrible scene at the front door without so much as a murmur? If Emily had not seen one of them shuffle an old, shabby carpet slipper just then, she might have wondered if they were even alive. But the worst thing was that they all seemed to be looking right through her as if she were not even there, as if *she* had become a shadow too!

She had no more than made this new, startling, and frightening discovery, however, than she made another one of an entirely different nature. Directly ahead of her, at the foot of the staircase, sat a round table laid with a magnificent, full-skirted red velvet cloth. Its heavy gold fringe barely brushed against the worn carpet, as if it were afraid to touch such a shabby relic. On this splendid setting rested a large bowl of cut crystal, so brilliant it twinkled like a star in the dusky parlor. And in the bowl lay a neatly arranged miniature mound of her favorite Christmas treat—puffy, tempting, tantalizing, delicious pink-and-white-striped peppermint drops! It almost seemed that they had been placed there just for Emily. Forgetting everything, she set down her travelling bag and reached out her hand.

Snap! Another hand, thin and cold as six feet under, flicked around her wrist. "Those are not placed there for the benefit of charity brats!" hissed Mrs. Meeching. Behind her, Aunt Twice gave a fainting gasp.

With wide eyes still fastened on the peppermint drops, Emily picked up her bag and numbly followed after Aunt Twice.

THREE

Tilly

They did not go up the broad oak stairway at all, so it seemed that not only was Emily not to have her old room again, but she was not even to have a room near it. Where then? she wondered. Aunt Twice had made a direct turn to the left instead, and they had now entered the dining room.

But how changed it was from the last time Emily had seen it! No longer did a cut glass chandelier twinkle over a dining set of the finest polished, carved mahogany. Now a single lamp threw a dim, trembling light over two rows of unpainted wooden chairs standing like stiff sentries around a long table that looked as if it had seen endless service in a pauper's kitchen. Each chair guarded a thick crockery bowl and plate, a tin cup and spoon set on an unwholesome brown oilcloth cover. Aunt Twice hurried past them without a glance, and Emily scurried after her. She could still feel Mrs. Meeching's eyes piercing her back as she followed

Aunt Twice through a heavy swinging door into an enormous, bleak kitchen.

Of course, in Emily's earlier position of pampered visitor, she had never entered this kitchen, but she could not believe it had ever looked as it did now, as if everything in it had been dipped in a bucket of grey paint. A gas lamp glared at her coldly from across a grey iron sink. Two grey iceboxes, one large as a wardrobe and secured by a grim padlock, loomed in a corner. On the stove, a thin, grey, watery soup bubbled in an ugly grey enamel cauldron. It was, without doubt, the dreariest kitchen Emily had ever seen.

But all the while she was taking in the kitchen, another pair of eyes was taking *her* in. The eyes, a washed-out blue, looked as if they had been sunk in dishwater for a very long time. They belonged to a lank-haired girl thirteen or fourteen years of age, whose sallow complexion somehow reflected the dismal color of the kitchen. She was sitting at one of two unpainted pine tables, polishing her fingernails on a dirty rag.

As Aunt Twice threw off her coat and hat, quickly lifting down a long muslin apron from a nail on the wall, the girl stood up and produced a wide yawn. Casting curious sideways glances in Emily's direction, she sidled over to the stove and began to stir the soup with a large iron spoon.

"Soup's done," she said dully, gazing into the pot.

"Thank you, Tilly," replied Aunt Twice. She finished tying on her apron with fumbling, distraught fingers. "I'll manage now."

Emily was beginning to wonder if her aunt had forgotten all about her as she stood waiting with her travelling bag at her feet. But apron now on, Aunt Twice hurried back to her. She had an arm out as if to put it around Emily, but a glance over her shoulder showed her that Tilly's eyes were locked on them in an inquisitive stare. With a strange tightening of the lips, Aunt Twice quickly dropped her arm.

"Tilly," she said, "this is my niece, Emily. Emily, this is Tilly, who helps with the cooking and cleaning and lives here as well."

Emily immediately dropped a polite curtsy. "How do you do, Tilly."

Tilly, looking somewhat surprised that anyone should be addressing her in this manner, herself dropped a muttered "How do" into the soup. A blink of an eye later, however, she was once again examining Emily with a sly look of appraisal.

"Tilly, I haven't time, so will you please show Emily to her room? It will be the small one next to mine. Then show her where she may wash. You may go with Tilly, Emily." Even as she was speaking, the harried, frightened look Emily was now coming to expect had returned to Aunt Twice's face. She pulled out a ring of keys, which hung by a chain to the belt of her dress. Selecting one key with nervous fingers, she hastened to the large icebox and inserted the key into the heavy padlock.

A moment later, Emily found herself looking into the most magnificent display of food she had ever seen, even at Mama's and Papa's grandest parties. There was a large ham, a golden roasted turkey, fresh green salads, a bowl of plump red strawberries, a vanilla cream cake all decorated with pale green flutings and flowers, orange and lemon jellies, a chocolate custard, small cakes and cookies of all descriptions—almost everything imaginable. So that unappetizing soup on the stove was not the only food served for dinner after all, Emily decided with relief. She could hardly pull her eyes away from the icebox.

Tilly laid her spoon on the stove. "Quits y'r gawping and come with me!" She darted a cunning look sideways to see how this command would sit with Aunt Twice. But if Aunt Twice, who was busy pulling a spun-sugar confection from the ice box, heard Tilly, she gave no sign of it.

Though nearly twice Emily's size, Tilly made no offer to help her with the travelling bag, so once again she picked it up herself. She had no idea yet where she was to go, but even though Aunt Twice had not taken her upstairs, she still supposed there must be a room somewhere in the house for her. She turned toward the dining room door.

"Servants' quarters ain't that way," Tilly said. She

sauntered to another door directly across from the one to the dining room, flung it open, and stood waiting for Emily with a strange glint in her eyes.

"Servants' quarters! Well, if she had to scrub sinks, scour pots, and empty slop jars, wasn't that what Emily had become now, a servant? And didn't that mean a room in the cellar? Her heart felt as if it were sinking right down to the toes of her white, high-button shoes as she made her journey across the kitchen toward Tilly.

"You mights as well get y'r peepers off the big icebox what's got a lock on it," Tilly said as soon as they had entered a dark, dank entry, thickly perfumed by the contents of an open garbage pail. "It ain't for you!"

Emily swallowed the dry lump that had risen in her throat. "J-j-just like the peppermints," she whispered.

"You knows 'bout them things already?" Tilly asked. She giggled into her hand as if she found this thought enormously amusing.

By now they had started down a long, steep flight of stone steps, feebly lit by a tiny speck of gaslight at the bottom. Down, down went Tilly without a backward glance, and bump, bump went Emily, following behind. All she could think of right then was saving herself from hurtling downward and breaking every bone in her body.

She reached the bottom step at last and found they were in a room much larger than the entry above, but equally dark and dank. And though not reeking with the scent of garbage, it was heavy with the must and mold of a quarter of a century. From this room, dark passages branched off in two directions. Tilly turned to the left. She had gone only a few feet, however, when a slight scratching sound overhead caused her to hesitate and look up.

"Rat," she said matter-of-factly. "You either gets used to 'em"—she looked back at Emily with lips compressed into a wicked grin—"or you doesn't!"

Emily clutched her travelling bag more tightly. On they went, passing one door after another, all firmly closed. Except for the hollow sounds made by their footsteps on the stone floor and the bumping of the bag against Emily's knees, there was a deep underground silence all around them. But as Tilly started to turn at last through the open door of a very tiny room, a faint sound, as if something or some*one* were sighing, came from behind another closed door at the far end of the passageway. This particular door, unlike all the others, had a small square window in the center. The sound so startled and terrified Emily that she let go her bag, and it fell to the floor with a jarring crash.

Tilly whirled on her. "What was that for?" she said crossly. "You scairt me out o' my wits!"

"Th-th-that room," Emily stammered. "I heard a *sound* come from there, I think."

Tilly shrugged. "No doubts you did. That's the Remembrance Room. Someone in there remembering what it done wrong."

"Remembrance Room?" Emily repeated dimly. There was a chilling sound about the words. "It did wrong? *Who* did wrong?"

"One o' the old ones, o' course. Who did you thinks?" Tilly's flat nose wrinkled with disgust at Emily's stupidity.

The old ones, those sad shadows huddled in the chairs in the parlor! What new horrors was she still to discover at Sugar Hill Hall?

"Took a peppermint most likely," Tilly went on in a dreamy kind of voice. "That's what they always does. Hmmm, wonder which one? Most o' them ain't got the nerve."

"C-c-couldn't you knock and find out?" Emily's voice was quavering. "Perhaps you could let the person out."

"And has *myself* tossed in?" Tilly shrivelled her with a pale blue stare. "Not likely! Mrs. Meeching puts 'em in. Mrs. Meeching puts 'em out. I ain't got the key anyways. Us'll most likely find out at dinner who it is, not as how I cares all that much. Now you hurries and drops off your gear. Us can't take all night."

The gaslight Tilly lit as they entered the small room was so weak, the wonder was it gave any light at all. But as Emily took off her coat and tam-o'-shanter, she could see all she needed to of the room that was to be hers.

It was so tiny that, except for a sliver of a window high in the wall, it might well have been intended for nothing more than a storage room. And if the future inhabitant did not gather this, further notice was given by the lack of furnishings. The stone floor was bare and so were the walls, but for a row of thin nails that jutted out like bones from a fish skeleton, intended for use as clothes hangers. All the room provided by way of comfort was an iron cot, a small brown chest of drawers with gaping wounds that revealed at least half a dozen coats of paint below, and over this last a small oval mirror as full of cracks as a dropped egg.

After the one quick glance needed to explore this cubicle, Emily folded her coat and laid it neatly on the cot with her tam-o'-shanter. She had decided that no matter what the condition of her new life, or how ugly her room, she would follow the rules set down by Mama and Mrs. Leslie, including not only politeness and good manners, but neatness and cleanliness as well. She had no sooner put the tam-o'-shanter down, however, than Tilly, without even asking leave, snatched it up again and jammed it on her own head at a rakish forward angle. Then she began to pose before the mirror, so taken with her cracked image that she seemed to have forgotten all about the need to hurry.

"Please, Tilly, where may I wash?" Emily asked, certain that Tilly had forgotten about *that*, too.

Tilly jerked a thumb over her shoulder. "Two doors back down the passageway that way. And see you doesn't take all day 'bout it!"

The cold, damp, stone washroom would hardly give anyone the desire to "take all day 'bout it." Emily was happy to escape it as quickly as possible, her fingers still stinging from the icy water provided by the cracked enamel pitcher. When she returned to the room, however, Tilly no longer had the hat on her head. Instead she was holding it in one hand and with the other stroking the fur as if it were a small animal.

"It's nice," she said dreamily. "Where's it come from? A rabbit?"

"No," replied Emily.

"What then?" Tilly persisted.

"An—an ermine," Emily said. Then she promptly wished she had thought to say *weasel*, which didn't sound nearly so royal.

Tilly's pale eyelashes flew upward. "Oooh!"

"You—you may borrow it any time you like, Tilly," Emily said quickly.

"Mights as well," Tilly replied. "It don't look too good on *you* with y'r hair all hanging 'round in strings."

Emily thought this a remarkably ungracious acceptance speech, but decided it would be best to say no more about it. She simply remained perched on the edge of the cot until Tilly should be ready to leave.

Tilly continued stroking the hat a moment longer, and then looked up at Emily slyly. "I bets you has lots o' pretty things in that bag. Ain't you going to open it now?"

Emily hesitated. The key to the bag was hanging on the gold chain around her neck, along with her locket, where Mrs. Leslie had put it so she would be certain not to lose it. She would have loved right then to open her travelling bag and pull out her warm pink shawl. She was shivering in her silk dress. But the look on Tilly's face, together with the sudden recollection of what *else* lay in the suitcase, made her settle instead on telling a lie, the first she had ever told. She drew a deep breath. "I—I haven't the key, Tilly. My—my aunt has it."

To Emily's relief, Tilly never noticed the hesitation. "You is going to let me look at 'em some time else then, ain't you?" she said, stroking the fur. Then without waiting for a reply, she went right on, smooth as syrup, into, "Us ought to be friends, Emily. I means, us both being orphings, and all that."

Emily had already determined that she would try to be as friendly to Tilly as possible, but she was not at all certain that they could actually be *friends,* even if they were both "orphings." A friend was someone she could trust, like Theodora, who had been her best friend and with whom she had shared all her confidences. How could anyone share a confidence with Tilly? Emily was greatly relieved, therefore, that Tilly did not seem to expect a lifelong pledge of devotion at that moment. Instead she thrust the tam-o'-shanter into her apron pocket (making Emily wonder if she would ever see it again), and started for the door.

Emily hurried after her as she stumped back down the passageway. "Tilly?" She shuddered as she glanced back over her shoulder. "What—what about the Remembrance Room?"

"Well, what 'bout it?" snapped Tilly.

"When is the person going to be let out?"

"Oh, *it*," said Tilly indifferently. "Depends on what it done. After dinner most likely. But if it done something terrible, like snitching *two* peppermints, then it gets to spend the night."

Spend the night in the Remembrance Room! The thought was so horrifying that Emily failed to notice Tilly stopping at the top of the stairs until she felt a sharp pinch on her arm. The squeak she let out was cut in half by Tilly's hand clapped tightly over her mouth.

"Shhh! That's to remind you us is to be equals. Mrs. Meeching says so. So no nanky-panky from y'r aunt, *or else!* You gets that?"

The hand remained over Emily's mouth until this entire message was delivered, so that when she felt another even sharper pinch on her arm, there was no squeak heard at all. This seemed very odd behavior from one who had so recently proclaimed she wanted the two "orphings" to be friends, but gave one more reason why Emily felt she had to be wary of Tilly.

They entered the bleak grey kitchen, which seemed surprisingly cheerful after the trip below. Perhaps this was because one of the two tables had been covered with gold-rimmed china bowls and platters heaped with green lettuces, red strawberries, and orange and yellow jellies, all making the room look as if a garden had sprung up suddenly in its midst. Aunt Twice stood at the table busily decorating the platters with frilly bits of parsley and wafer-thin slices of lemon. Was it possible that this beautiful food was for them after all? Emily wondered.

But Tilly stumped right past this table to the second one, which bore only a large, sickly brown basket of bread lumps, not too recently baked if slight tinges of grey-green here and there were any indication. Emily felt a strange, sinking feeling arrive suddenly in the pit of her stomach.

"What has kept you girls so long? You know you must be on time for serving, Tilly." Aunt Twice wiped her hands nervously on her apron.

"Oh, 'tweren't me! Emily took such a long time washing," replied Tilly blandly as she wheeled a serving cart from the corner and hoisted the bread basket onto it.

Knowing the washroom down below as Aunt Twice did, Emily thought, she must surely have had some doubts about the truthfulness of this statement, but she pressed her lips together and kept silent. So, for that matter, did Emily, for if she had not learned already what was and what was not expected of her, a stinging spot on her arm was now there to remind her.

"Well, hurry, do hurry *please!* Oh dear, Emily, darl—" Aunt Twice caught herself. "Emily, you'll need an apron. Tilly, do let her borrow one of yours, will you? Then come, please, and help me with the pot."

Glowering at Emily, Tilly thumped to the wall and retrieved from a nail an apron as greasy as the one she had on. "Why can't *she* help with it?"

Aunt Twice sighed. "Tilly, compare the size of Emily to the size of the pot. We would have soup all over the floor, and then what would we do for dinner?"

"Well, she can very well clean it then!" grumped Tilly. She wheeled the serving cart to the stove with a sour look on her face.

As Emily struggled to tie on the too-long, ugly apron, Aunt Twice and Tilly laboriously lifted from the stove to the cart both the huge grey pot and a steaming teakettle. Next to the kettle Aunt Twice set a small green china bowl containing a white muslin bag not much larger than a postage stamp. Attached to one corner of the bag was a short length of string. Emily wondered at the purpose of this odd little bag, but any question she might have had about it was cut off by a sharp sniff from Tilly.

"All right, you can come 'long now. Ain't too helpless to push the cart, I trusts!"

Her long apron dragging on the floor, Emily quickly placed her pale hands next to Tilly's rough red ones on the serving cart, and they pushed it through the swinging door into the dining room. The first thing Emily noticed was that a crockery bowl, plate, tin cup, and spoon were ominously missing from one place halfway down the long table. She tried not to think about it.

Tilly darted a quick look at the cheerless grandfather clock ticking mournfully in a corner. "Us hasn't no time to shilly-shally. Mrs. Meeching likes 'em served 'fore they enters. So *if* you thinks you has the muscle"— this with a heavy note of disgust—"you holds up the bowls whilst I pours."

Emily picked up a bowl promptly and managed to hold it steadily as Tilly ladled the unappetizing soup into it. She looked grudgingly pleased that Emily might actually be of some use after all.

"You knows," Tilly said, almost cheerfully, " 'fore you come, it were y'r aunt what poured, whilst I done the bowls. Pouring ain't easy. It's a step up in life, you might say."

Emily tried to give Tilly a friendly smile over the soup bowl, although it was difficult for her to imagine anyone being pleased about such a promotion.

"O' course," Tilly went on, "I done it once or twice before when y'r aunt were ailing, and Kipper stuck 'round to help."

"Who is Kipper?" asked Emily.

"He's a boy. His pa owns a fish shop. Kipper delivers the fish and helps 'bout the place." Tilly paused to give Emily an appraising look. " 'Bout y'r age, I'd say. Anyways, you'll see him." She snickered into her hand. "Can't miss him much!"

The nature of this reply gave Emily another sinking feeling in the middle of her stomach. She suspected that this boy might be just one more horror she had to deal with. Did he specialize in nasty tricks? Can't miss him much—it sounded ominous!

"There, soup's done," Tilly said. "Now us pours the hot water into the cups."

It seemed to Emily that they had really just finished pouring hot water into the *bowls*. She has never before heard of a meal that was so awash in hot water.

"Did Aunt Twice pour for that, too?" she asked.

Tilly's eyebrows rose. "Is that what you calls y'r aunt, Aunt Twice? What kind o' name is that?"

"Mama was Aunt Twice's sister, and Papa was *Uncle* Twice's brother," Emily explained. "That made them my aunt and uncle two times over." She wondered how Tilly would act at this mention of an *Uncle* Twice. So far not one word had been mentioned about him. Emily would have questioned Aunt Twice, but her aunt had been so preoccupied and so distraught, she had not dared. Besides, wasn't it up to Aunt Twice to tell *her?* She watched Tilly's face anxiously for a sign.

Tilly's brows knit together over pale, blank eyes as if straining Emily's explanation through her brain was far more than she could manage. Then, to Emily's terrible disappointment, she skipped right back to the first question.

"Well, y'r aunt done the hot water, too. *You* couldn't, howsumever!" Tilly accompanied this pronouncement with a disdainful wrinkle of her flat nose. "Not just 'cause it's heavy, but it ain't easy not to slosh it over the edges and all. *You* gets to deliver the bread lumps, one to a customer."

Emily began setting the hard, moldy bread on the tin plates. "What about the little bag?" she asked.

"Oh, that's their little treat. *You'll* see," Tilly replied mysteriously, and placed the small green bowl at the head of the table. Just then, the grandfather clock began to toll the hour, and she sucked in her breath. "Us has to hurry, or us'll get caught!"

Emily quickly set a bread lump on the last plate and started at once for the kitchen.

"Sssst!" Tilly clamped a firm hand around her arm.

"Us has to stay in the dining room case they wants more. Quick, over here!"

Tilly had no sooner spoken than the doors from the parlor flew open and Mrs. Meeching entered the dining room, gliding silently across the floor as if she had no legs at all. Her black skirt hissed faintly around her ankles. Behind her appeared the cozy Mrs. Plumly, her knitting needles clicking away busily.

Emily began to shiver as if a draught of cold air had blown across the floor. But Mrs. Meeching never even glanced in her direction, as if she were nothing more than a parlor shadow. Mrs. Meeching went at once to the head of the table, where she stood, hands folded, like a pillar of black frost. Mrs. Plumly placed herself at the chair across the table, needles clicking at full speed.

Then the old people began to drift through the doors. Eyes dull, hands shaking, legs trembling, they shuffled unsteadily across the floor in shabby shoes and carpet slippers. Their poor, sad, wrinkled faces were as lifeless as when they had stared at Emily across the parlor. Silently, each one found a place at the table.

As soon as the scraping of chairs, chillingly noted by Mrs. Meeching, had ended, she picked up the small green bowl containing the tiny muslin bag and raised her eyes heavenward.

"For what we are about to receive, let us be truly grateful." She allowed a few moments for this thin blessing to arrive at its destination, and then went on. "Today, Mr. Figg will start the tea bag. If you please, Mrs. Quirk?"

A little muslin bag filled with a few tea leaves— so that's what it was! With wide eyes, Emily watched the green bowl handed to Mrs. Quirk, and then on down the line of old, trembling hands to Mr. Figg. Carefully as his frail, thin hands would allow him, Mr. Figg lifted up the string and dipped the tea bag into his tin cup of hot water. A second passed. Two seconds passed. Mrs. Meeching sniffed audibly, and bowl and bag were handed to the next old person at the table.

Around the table travelled the tea bag, dipped into a cup at every place, except where Mrs. Plumly and Mrs. Meeching sat. And, of course, the place where no one sat at all. Long before the bag reached the last person, it must have left not the slightest shade of color in the cup, much less any taste of tea.

Even beyond this pitiful sideshow, it was the most dismal, silent dinner that Emily had ever witnessed. There were no sounds of laughter, no conversation of any kind. All that could be heard was the *tick, tick* of the clock, the *click, click* of Mrs. Plumly's knitting needles, and an occasional weak *ping* of a tin spoon hitting against a bowl. No one finished any soup, and no one so much as tasted a bread lump. So, of course, when Mrs. Meeching asked if anyone cared for more, no one raised a hand. Thus the meal ended. Preceded by Mrs. Meeching and Mrs. Plumly, the old people shuffled silently out of the dining room.

Who was to eat all that delectable food Aunt Twice was preparing in the kitchen? Emily wondered. But she did not need to wonder long. A few moments later, the kitchen door burst open, and Aunt Twice flew out. Her apron whirling out around her, she rolled another serving cart laden with the food in question to a third door that led from the dining room. As she opened the door to pass through, there was just enough time for Emily to see a small, cozy room with red velvet chairs drawn up to a low table set for two before a crackling fire in the fireplace. A lace cloth covered the table, and on it were two settings of gleaming silver, china and crystal. And before the door slammed shut, who did Emily see settling themselves comfortably in the chairs but Mrs. Meeching and Mrs. Plumly!

"All right, now you knows, so quits y'r gawping," said Tilly. "Us still has to eat and do up."

Eat? Emily shuddered as she watched Tilly pour all the ugly, untouched bread back into the basket from the plates, not to mention pouring Mrs. Meeching's and Mrs. Plumly's untouched soup back into the soup pot. Surely, Emily tried to tell herself, Aunt Twice had left something good for her in the kitchen, something to tempt her appetite. But when she and Tilly rolled the serving cart back into the kitchen, all Emily found staring back at her were two bare tables, a sink piled mountain-high with dirty pots and pans, and the large icebox tightly padlocked. Every bit of lettuce green, strawberry red, and jelly orange and yellow had been swept away, and not so much as a sprig of parsley remained.

All too soon, Emily found herself seated with Tilly at a kitchen table, facing a bowl of grey, watery soup and a large lump of moldy bread. She had managed one taste of each article, and that was all.

"Sorry if the food ain't dainty 'nough for you," said Tilly, gulping a large spoonful of soup. But then she added in a surprisingly kind tone, "You eats the bread, leastways. What everyone don't eat today, everyone gets tomorrow!"

"Couldn't we throw it away?" Emily asked. She remembered that, after all, there *was* a garbage can in the kitchen entry.

"Not *me!*" Tilly flicked a patch of grey-green from her bread with a practiced fingernail. "Everything 'round here got a number on it, not just the peppermints." She narrowed her pale eyes knowingly at Emily.

Nonetheless, Emily could eat no more. She simply sat and watched in amazement as Tilly put away two bowls of the dismal soup and at least three lumps of the ancient bread.

Any kindliness Tilly might have felt at the supper table, however, met sudden death when it came to the sink. Tilly had been promised that Emily would do the soup pot, and thus Emily *did* the soup pot (which she had to scour and scrape from atop a wooden lettuce crate, being too small to reach the high sink), not to mention bowls and plates, tin cups and spoons, and a dozen more pots and pans, before, under Tilly's baleful eyes, she was rescued by Aunt Twice.

It hardly seemed possible to Emily that it was only the hour of her usual bedtime when she stumbled down below to her room, her mind numbed by the mountain of dirty dishes, her hands raw from soaking and scrubbing, and one arm stinging from another pinch given her privately by Tilly as they both left the kitchen.

FOUR

A Disturbing Explanation

Once in her cellar room, Emily collapsed onto her cot and stared at the tiny sliver high up in the wall that was to be her only window. Forever? she wondered. She was too weary to unpack her travelling bag and take out her nightdress. She was even too weary to pull off her clothes. She could not think of a bone in her body that did not ache, and she felt so *empty,* though not really hungry. How could she ever be hungry for the ugly food in that ugly kitchen?

Suddenly she began to shiver so hard she could not stop. She was cold and tired, but more than that, she began to remember all that had happened to her, especially where she was now, in a small dank room of stone deep in the ground, with horror overhead and horror just outside the door—the Remembrance Room with its sighing, moaning inhabitant! What kind of evil mind could invent such cruel punishment for a sad old person who had done nothing more than take a peppermint? Though still in her dress, Emily was ready to throw herself under the bedclothes and pull them up over her head to hide from the terrors of her room. Then suddenly she heard a faint knock at her door.

"Who—who is it?" she asked, frightened.

"Aunt Twice," came the whispered reply.

Aunt Twice! Emily ran to the door and threw it open. Silent as a shadow, Aunt Twice slipped in, carefully closing the door behind her. Then, without another word, she took Emily in her arms.

"Oh, Aunt Twice!" Emily sobbed. "I thought you would never come!"

"My poor darling child!" Aunt Twice said. "What a cruel life you've come to! But you are being brave, and I am so proud of you. Still, you must continue to remember, much as I would wish it were not so, that

this house and its owner"—Aunt Twice shuddered—
"must come first. They must come before *everything*."

"I *will* remember," Emily promised. "But oh, Aunt
Twice, who are all the old people? Why are *they* here?"

"They are people no one wants," Aunt Twice replied gently. "Their families can no longer look after
them, or sadly and cruelly, no longer want them. This
is an old people's home that you've come to, Emily."

"Are all old people's homes like this one? Must
they all come to such a place?" Emily asked.

"No, Emily. There are pleasant, kind homes, but
this is not one of them. This is an evil place—wicked and
evil. It is only the *uncaring* who leave their old people
behind here."

"Oh, Aunt Twice!" Emily cried. "Can nothing be
done about them?"

"Nothing!" said Aunt Twice with tight lips.

Emily shuddered. "It was such a mournful dinner-
time. Why can't they share some of the beautiful food
in the big ice box?"

Aunt Twice stiffened. "You must not ask any questions about the food, Emily. I know how horrible the
food is for them, and for you too, but you must never
touch any of the other, even if you think no one is
watching. Everything here is numbered. Everything is
accounted for."

The very thing Tilly had said! Emily thought. But
her aunt had told her she was to ask no more questions

about the food, so there was nothing more to say about it. At any rate, another pressing question had jumped into her mind. "Aunt Twice, *you're* not an old person. Why are *you* here?"

"Because I am a prisoner," replied Aunt Twice simply.

"A prisoner? But you came to meet me at the train station," Emily said. "And you aren't in chains."

Aunt Twice smiled a grim smile. "There are other ways of being a prisoner, Emily. Someone's very life depends on my serving the owner of Sugar Hill Hall!"

Someone's very life! *"Who?"* Emily breathed.

Aunt Twice hesitated. "I—I cannot tell you. I *cannot!"*

"But Aunt Twice," Emily blurted out, "can't—can't *Uncle Twice* come to help you? Where *is* he?"

Aunt Twice's face turned ashen. "Hush, child, hush!" Her eyes darted around the small room as if pursued by some deadly horror. "The walls here have eyes and ears! You must never speak of him again. Never! You must think of him as—as *dead!* Will you promise that?"

Think of Uncle Twice as dead—did that mean he was really alive? Questions tumbled wildly in Emily's head. But Aunt Twice had said that she must *never* speak of him again and had asked for her promise. Numbly, Emily nodded her head.

Aunt Twice looked as if she might be going to say

something more. Her mouth opened suddenly, but then just as suddenly snapped shut. And Emily knew then that it was locked upon its secret terrors as tightly as the door of the Remembrance Room. If she was ever going to find any answers to her questions, it would have to be on her own.

After a moment, the frozen expression on Aunt Twice's face softened into a sad, dim smile. She reached out to stroke Emily's head gently. "Oh, those beautiful golden braids! Well, at least we can trim what is left so you won't look like such a straggly little waif." She dipped a hand into the pocket of her plain brown calico dress and pulled out a pair of scissors.

A short while later, after a snip here and a snip there, Emily looked at herself in the cracked mirror. Although far from beautiful, the haircut was certainly an improvement over the one provided earlier. Emily managed a smile at her reflection to please Aunt Twice.

"You poor, tired child, not even in your nightdress yet," Aunt Twice said. "And you haven't yet unpacked your travelling bag. I thought you might have done so when you came down with Tilly."

"I—I wasn't certain I should," Emily stammered.

"But why not?" asked Aunt Twice.

"Because—" Emily hesitated. "Because there is something in it I'm not certain Tilly should see." She pulled the gold chain from her dress and quickly unhooked the key, hoping that Aunt Twice would not notice the locket. If she did and saw the picture of herself and Uncle Twice, she would most certainly want the picture destroyed. But, with all interest on the key, she seemed not to notice the locket.

Emily unlocked her travelling bag and reached into a tiny secret compartment in the silk lining. From it she pulled out a small white paper packet. Then she opened the packet and poured its contents into Aunt Twice's hand—twenty pure gold coins!

"Papa's lawyer, Mr. Dowling, gave them to me before I left," Emily explained. "I suspect he thought I might need the money before my allowance could start coming to you from Papa's will."

"Oh, dear child!" Aunt Twice cried. "Don't you know? Your papa died a pauper! He lost everything in the sudden failure of his company. Mr. Dowling wrote me that there *is* no money coming."

"N-n-no money coming?" said Emily, confused. "Then—then where did Mr. Dowling get the gold coins?"

"I would guess from his own pocket," murmured Aunt Twice softly. "But with all expectations now ended, there is even greater reason for these gold coins to be protected. You were right not to show them to Tilly. But where can you keep them? *My* room is not safe."

Her eyes searched the room swiftly. Then at last

she gave a small cry of triumph. Lifting up a corner of the thin mattress on the cot, she made a tiny slit at the seam of ticking with her scissors. One by one, she slipped the coins through. Then, with a needle and thread found in her pocket, she stitched up the opening with trembling fingers.

She had no sooner finished this task, however, when a sound hardly more than that of a whisper of air outside the door made her jerk up her head and stiffen. For a moment she stood with staring eyes, motionless as a mouse accustomed to the soft, secret approach of a cat's paws, or a snake's belly. Then, with a finger to her lips as a signal for Emily to be silent, she crept slowly to the door and flung it open.

"*Tilly!* What are you doing?" For all its sternness, Aunt Twice's voice was quivering.

"I just wondered what you was doing," whined Tilly. "You never comes to talk to *me* at night."

Aunt Twice sighed. "I didn't know you wanted me to, Tilly, and we are ordinarily both too weary at night. But I have not seen my niece in years, and so I wished to talk to her about her dear departed mother and father."

"You never talks to me 'bout *my* dear departed ma and pa," said Tilly, pouting. "Leastways, my departed *pa*. My ma just upped and died."

"Tilly," said Aunt Twice patiently, "your mother died when you were born, and your father left you soon after. But that was years and years ago. Emily has only just lost her mother and father in a terrible accident."

"I doesn't care," said Tilly stubbornly. "I wants to talk 'bout 'em. Us orphings is supposed to be equals. I heard Mrs. Meeching say so. If you talks 'bout *her* ma and pa, you has to talk 'bout mine, too!"

Aunt Twice stiffened at the mention of Mrs. Meeching's name. "When did you want to talk about them, Tilly?"

"Right now!"

"It's very late," Aunt Twice said. "Wouldn't tomorrow night do just as well?"

Tilly thought this over. "Well, long as you doesn't forget. Hey! Ain't that Emily's bag open? She promised as how she'd 'low me to see her pretty things."

"I'm only taking out my nightdress now, Tilly," Emily said. She remembered that her tam-o'-shanter was still in Tilly's apron pocket, where, for all she knew, it had taken up permanent residence. "We can look at them tomorrow. I promise we will."

There was more thought from Tilly. "Well, long as you promises, I guess *'tis* late."

"Yes, of course it is," said Aunt Twice quickly. "That's a sensible girl, Tilly. Now come along, and we'll go *together* to our rooms. Good night, Emily!" She closed the door without so much as a backward look.

They never had talked about Mama and Papa, but Emily already had come to accept the way Aunt Twice must behave now, so she was not startled at being left so suddenly. Still, this did not make it any easier to be left alone once again in her cold, stony, silent underground cell. Silent, that is, except for strange scratching sounds overhead. Rats? she wondered. Quickly she threw off her clothes and slipped into her nightdress.

Before she turned down the gaslight, however, she opened her locket to study the photographs inside it. Shadows danced eerily over the tiny figures—Mama, Papa, Aunt Twice, Uncle Twice. Tall, slender Uncle Twice with the golden mustaches and the twinkling blue eyes! As with Mama and Papa, was a photograph all Emily would ever have to remember him by? Shivering, she finally turned down the light, jumped into her cot, and pulled the skimpy coverlet tight up around her face. She hoped she would fall asleep at once, yet no sooner would she close her eyes than terrifying shapes danced across her eyelids, making them fly open.

As she stared into the darkness, questions began again to whirl through her head. She thought of the mountains of delicious food in the locked icebox. Surely, two ladies, even with the most enormous appetites, could not consume so much food. Everything numbered—everything accounted for, so surely nothing would be lightly tossed away either. Who *did* eat it then?

But the one burning question that returned over and over had to do with Uncle Twice. She was to think of him as dead—*why?* Could he be the one whose life depended on Aunt Twice serving the dread Mrs. Meeching? Or was the life Aunt Twice so desperately protected one Emily as yet knew nothing about, so she was to think of her uncle as dead because—because he had become as evil as this mansion. Because *he* was the depraved mind behind all this horror, and not Mrs. Meeching. Well, after all, he had bought Sugar Hill Hall, hadn't he? Wasn't he the owner? Emily tried to sweep these ugly thoughts from her mind, but they stuck firm and would not be swept away.

Of one thing, however, she was becoming certain. There were terrible secrets locked up in Sugar Hill Hall, and somehow she had the feeling that the key to all of them lay with Uncle Twice. But where was he? Would she ever find out? Whom could she ask? Not Aunt Twice, she now knew. Her aunt was much too frightened to reveal anything, holding a life in her hands. Tilly then? She probably knew little, and what she did know she would not likely tell Emily. So whatever Emily discovered, she would have to manage on her own.

How she could possibly discover anything, she had no idea. It would take all her strength and wits just to keep from becoming another shadow like the old people. But she would *not* become one! she told herself fiercely. Nor would she ever let Mrs. Meeching see tears in *her* eyes. *Never!*

But all this bravery would have to start tomorrow. Tonight she was a cold, lonely, frightened girl, away from the only home she had ever known. She had lost her mama and papa, and there was nothing to look forward to but grey soup and moldy bread, and odd Tilly for her only friend. The sounds of her tears and sobbing, when they came, were deeply buried in her small, hard pillow, because she had not forgotten, even in all her misery, that the walls had eyes and ears.

FIVE

Kipper

Emily's favorite ornament on the Christmas tree had always been a pink, blue, and silver cardboard gondola pulled by two white glass swans with silvery spun-glass tails. As a tiny girl, she would often sit and stare at it for minutes on end, forgetting all her new Christmas gifts. That night she dreamed about her swans, but rather than floating amidst a hundred sparkling ornaments and twinkling candles, they drifted alone around a tall, dark, lifeless tree.

All at once, as Emily watched them, they began to plummet to the ground. She reached out for them, but all her fingers closed around was ice-cold air. Sobbing, she crawled toward the tree, trying to gather the tiny bits of glass that had once been the swans, but all she could pick up in her hands was the two spun-glass tails. Then, as she held them, they began to squirm from her fingers, gliding into the dark tree like two small snakes with red ribbons around their tails. Emily began to scream. Then someone was shaking her, and she opened her eyes to find Tilly bending over her.

"What's all this 'bout, yelling y'r head off! Should o' et y'r bread last night what I told you to do. Anyways, you gets a second chance at it this morning. But you hurries up! Us has to get the coal for the stove 'fore the morning is half over." Yawning hugely, Tilly stumped out of the room.

Morning half over? How could it be morning at all when it was still black outside the sliver of a window? Was morning going to be the middle of the night from now on? Emily shivered as her toes touched the cold, damp, stone floor. She envied the ugly grey wool robe Tilly was wearing.

All Emily had in her travelling bag was a second silk dress, no more suitable for carrying coal or scrubbing dishes than the first. As it was also no warmer, she decided to wear the same dress again and save the other, though for *what* she could not imagine. But at least she now had her shawl out, and in time her trunks would come.

Trunks! Suddenly Emily remembered something Mrs. Leslie had packed in them—all Mama's jewels! What would happen if Tilly should see the diamond rings, the gold brooches, and Mama's beloved necklace of true pearls? Shouldn't they be hidden as well as the gold coins? But Emily had no time to think about that now. Fingers still aching from a hurried visit to the icy washroom, she quickly pulled on her clothes.

"Them white kid shoes and white stockings again!" said Tilly with disgust when she saw Emily. "Ain't you got nothing better to wear for work?"

"Not yet," Emily replied.

"Kid shoes and white stockings for carrying coal! Hmmmph!" grunted Tilly. "What a waste!"

They picked up empty tin buckets at the foot of the stairwell and clanked their way down the passageway to the coal room. This turned out to be directly next to the room Emily had tried not to think about all night.

"Is someone still in there, do you suppose?" she whispered to Tilly as they shovelled coal into their buckets.

"I don't got to suppose nothing," shouted Tilly in reply. "I *knows* it's in there. If it ain't out by night, then it gets to wait until after breakfast. If y'r in the kitchen, you might even get to see it brung out by Mrs. Meeching."

Emily wasn't at all excited about witnessing still another sideshow featuring one of the pitiful residents of Sugar Hill Hall. She *was* curious, however, about what kind of old person it might be who had dared to steal (accepting that Tilly was right about it) a peppermint. No, not *a,* but *two* peppermints! It would have to be someone much bigger and bolder than any of the others, she was certain.

"Quits y'r daydreaming!" Tilly's angry voice broke into her thoughts. "You ain't got more'n twenty coal lumps in y'r bucket. Oh well, *that's* probably more'n you can carry." Tilly sniffed. "Us might as well leave."

Aunt Twice was already in the kitchen starting up the stove when Emily stumbled in with her coal bucket behind Tilly. Preparations for the morning meal were underway. Although Emily had tried to strengthen her mind for the menu, she still suffered the same sinking feeling in her stomach when she saw on the stove the large graniteware pot filled now with a thin, colorless gruel, and on the table the familiar basket with the all-too-familiar lumps of last night's (if not last month's) bread.

She tried to keep her attention firmly away from the eggs, tub of yellow butter, pitcher of rich cream, and bowl heaped with oranges, bananas, and grapes, and crowned with the crisp green spikes of a fresh pine-apple, all laid out on the second table. But when the fragrances of bubbling coffee, sizzling bacon and sausages, and cinnamon buns baking in the oven wafted through the kitchen, there was no way that she could strengthen her mind to any of it. It was the first time in her life that she remembered being *really hungry,* and yet the moment she looked at the gruel and the bread lumps, her appetite vanished.

As for the old people's morning meal, enhanced by Mrs. Meeching's icy presence and a fog as gloomy as the one of the day before drifting past the windows, Emily felt it to be equally as dismal as their evening meal. Her own courage, which she had tried so hard to build up the night before, crumbled when Mrs. Meeching appeared.

Their dining room duties over, Emily again was only able to pick at her meal, although Tilly poured down three bowls of gruel and at least as many lumps of bread, which appeared to have grown even moldier overnight. And when Emily stood before the sink facing the piles of pots and pans, she felt as if she had never left them the night before.

"Do we get to rest now?" she asked hopefully when she finally climbed down from the lettuce crate.

Tilly turned disbelieving, dishwater-pale blue eyes in her direction. "What you gets to rest now is y'r knees on the kitchen floor whilst you rests y'r hands on a scrub brush. Then after that, you gets to help me with cleaning upstairs whilst y'r aunt does up for Mrs. M. and Mrs. P. This afternoon, by way of entertainment, you might say, you gets to do the laundry. After that, you la-de-das about waiting on table and scrubbing up, and *then* you falls into y'r cot. Whether you rests there or not's up to you!" A cast iron frying pan went heaving into a cupboard with a crash at this final pronouncement.

It wasn't long after that Tilly and Aunt Twice left the kitchen armed with brooms, mops, dust pans and sponges, and Emily was indeed down on her white-stockinged knees beside a bucket filled with grey, soapy water that looked astonishingly like the soup of the night before. Wearily, she began to scrub the floor. Before long, her knees felt as if the floor were trying to push its way right past them, and her hands as if the harsh soap had eaten its way to her bones. Along with only a brush and a bucket for company, and a dismal fog hunched up against the windows, Emily suddenly felt her resolve not to cry slipping away. She began to sing to try to cheer herself up.

> *"London Bridge is falling down,*
> *Falling down, falling down.*
> *London Bridge is falling down,*
> *My fair lady!"*

Piping out into the vast kitchen, her thin, small voice was hardly strong enough to reach the bleak, high ceiling overhead, but it helped her to scrub. "Falling down," sang Emily, at the same time suiting the action to the words. Down, brush! Down, brush! Even though the nursery rhyme soon lost all semblance of a tune, sung over and over as it was, it carried Emily across the floor to the stove on the far side of the kitchen. Then suddenly she stopped singing and scrubbing. At that moment, the loudest sound in the room was the thumping of her heart. She sensed that someone had entered the kitchen and was staring at her. Slowly, carefully, she turned her head to peer over her shoulder.

In the doorway stood an ordinary young boy in a well-worn, navy-blue wool jacket, and a somewhat disreputable green-and-white-striped muffler. He had materialized without either ringing a bell or knocking, bringing into the kitchen with him a newspaper-wrapped parcel, and an overpowering smell of fish as well.

But what made the boy not quite so ordinary after all was his ownership of the brightest head of curly red hair Emily had ever seen in her life. It shone like a patch of marigolds in the dreary grey kitchen. As for the rest of him, he was sturdy-looking, with a snub nose blanketed in freckles, eyes the color of the blue sea when the sun is on it, and cheeks so ruddy they seemed to be in competition with his hair to see which was the cheeriest. Bright red hair, a cheerful look, not to mention an overpowering smell of fish—it would be difficult to miss such a boy no matter where he was. *Can't miss seeing him!* Wasn't that what Tilly had said about a fishmonger's boy named Kipper?

The boy continued to dart curious looks at Emily over his shoulder as he set his parcel on a table, and then pulled off his coat and muffler. He hung both on a nail by the door as if the nail had his name on it. Then, pretending indifference, he picked up the parcel and strolled to the sink, whistling.

Emily felt strangely shy. She quickly returned to scrubbing the floor. Down, *brush!* Down, *brush!* She tried to keep her mind on her chore, but at last curiosity won out, and she stole a quick peek toward the sink. If she had been a little closer, she could have fallen right into the two big pools of blue that were the boy's eyes staring at her. Her cheeks flushed with embarrassment.

Her only consolation was that the boy's cheeks appeared to do the same. "My name's Kipper," he mumbled. "What's yours?"

"Emily."

"Emily? Then ain't you Mrs. Luccock's niece what was coming here?"

Emily nodded.

Then, with the stiff, self-conscious look he might

have worn had he just been told to look into a camera, Kipper said, "Well, howdy do, in which case."

Emily scrambled up from the floor and dropped a curtsy. "How do you do, Kipper."

In an instant, the frozen look on Kipper's face dissolved into a wide grin. "Dingus! Ain't anybody ever curtsied to *me* before, me not exactly being the King o' England. Pa would like it, curtsying and all that, even from someone what looks like a chimney sweep!"

Kipper's pleasure over the curtsy was so genuine that Emily couldn't even feel offended over this honest description of her appearance. Besides, she felt she must look *worse* than a chimney sweep with coal dust streaked from her chin to the tips of her once-white shoes, dirty water sloshed all over her silk dress, and the hem of her skirt black from dragging across the floor.

"You get here yesterday?" Kipper asked.

"Last night," replied Emily.

"And Tilly got you doing floors already, as well as carrying coal? *Wheeoo!*" Kipper whistled his sympathy.

"I scrub pots and pans, too," said Emily. "Tilly says we have to be equals."

"Well, you best be careful, or you'll end up more equal 'n Tilly, if you get my meaning." Kipper raised his eyebrows at Emily. "Anyways, speaking o' Tilly, you best get back to your 'London Bridge' whilst I tend to this fish." He started to unwrap the newspaper parcel. "Most times I just dump this in the icebox when Tilly's not here, nor your aunt, but today I got something special." He held up by the tail two huge, grey-speckled fish with dead, staring eyes.

Despite herself, Emily shuddered and crinkled her nose at the sight and the smell of these unattractive specimens.

Kipper shrugged ruefully. "They ain't the best-smelling things, I got to admit, being two or three days 'long in age. But Pa always sends 'em when he's got 'em left over, so the old ones can have something more than fish heads for their stew."

Fish head stew! What next? Emily was made speechless by the thought of those eyes staring dolefully up at her from her soup bowl. Whistling a tuneless tune, Kipper pulled a stout knife from his trousers pocket and began to scrape the fish. Fish scales flew out from the sink like a flurry of tiny silver coins. But suddenly, the hand wielding the knife froze in midair, and Kipper stood absolutely still, listening. Then he twisted his head with a jerk and stared at the dining room door. A moment later, Mrs. Meeching glided through the doorway as silently as day becoming night.

She crossed the kitchen, her small, cruel, unblinking eyes looking neither to right nor left. The fish scaler and small floor scrubber might very well have been tree stumps for all the attention she paid to them. But Emily knew that her eyes were watching them as much as if she had been staring right into them. She disappeared through the door leading below, and soon her footsteps were shrouded in silence.

"*Whooee!*" breathed Kipper. "Where's *she* going? To the pokey to get someone out?"

"Do you mean the Remembrance Room?" asked Emily.

"No other."

"I think so. Tilly said this is when—when *it* should come out."

"Well, Tilly ought to know," Kipper said matter of factly. "She's up on all them things." Then he lapsed into silence, absently scraping his knife across a fish.

A cloud seemed to have settled over the kitchen. Emily went back to her scrubbing. In any event, it was only a few minutes before Mrs. Meeching returned to the kitchen, and this time she was not alone.

Shuffling slowly behind her was an old, shriveled, white-haired little woman, as bent as a hairpin. Her trembling hands seemed no larger than bird claws, and her ankles were as thin as twigs. All told, she was hardly much bigger than Emily! With a mixture of horror and wonder, Emily watched this sad little parade pass into the dining room.

"Dingus, Emily!" Kipper exclaimed softly. "That's little Mrs. Poovey! If I never seen it with my own peepers, I wouldn't o' believed it. You know, none o' them says much, but that Mrs. Poovey, she ain't opened her mouth *once* what I know of. And most o' them cry, at first leastways, but she never even done that."

Kipper scratched his red curls with a finger still liberally coated with fish scales. "Well, I'll be a whale's tail, as Pa always says. Mrs. Poovey taking a peppermint! O' course, don't know if that's what she done, but like I said, if Tilly thinks so, ain't anyone got better credentuals for ferreting out news. Wonder now 'twas found out?"

From the eyes and ears in the walls, thought Emily. But she was suddenly frightened by the curious, sharp look in Kipper's eyes, too frightened to speak. She dipped her brush in the bucket and swept it intently across the floor. Then Kipper simply turned back to the sink and began to scrape his fish. Soon there was only the sound of scraping and brushing in the kitchen.

"Say, why ain't you back to singing your 'London Bridge'?" Kipper asked lightly.

"Because I only know one verse," Emily replied. "I just say it over and over."

"If you'll pardon my saying so, that ain't very exciting. *I* make up my own!" Kipper said proudly. "Would you like to hear some?"

Emily sat back on her heels, and nodded eagerly.

Then Kipper raised his knife and began waving it in the air like a conductor's baton as he started to sing.

"When I was young I went to sea,
Went to sea, went to sea,
The name of my ship was the Fiddle Dee Dee
My fair lady!

"Up came a storm and blew us all 'round,
Blew us all 'round, blew us all 'round,
Next I knew we was upside down,
My fair lady!

"Then right to the bottom went the Fiddle Dee Dee,
Fiddle Dee Dee, Fiddle Dee Dee,
But everyone was saved excepting me,
My fair lady!"

At this unexpected turn in the song, Emily began to giggle. Kipper grinned, and then dropping his voice so low it could have gone right through the floor to the cellar, he sang slowly and sonorously,

"Now bones is all that's left of me,
Left of me, left of me,
It's just me and the sea and the Fiddle Dee Dee,
My fair lady!"

By now Emily was giggling uncontrollably.
Kipper beamed. "Would you like me sing it again?"

Emily had no sooner nodded, however, than he said suddenly, "Whoops! No more o' that." He grimaced at her. "Morning, Tilly!"

Tilly had appeared before an angrily swinging dining room door, her hands planted on her hips. "What's this all 'bout?" she said, glowering at Kipper.

Kipper threw her a dazzling smile. "Don't be cross at us, Tilly!" he said in a wheedling voice. "I was just singing Emily a verse or two o' my 'London Bridge' whilst she was scrubbing and I was scraping. See, look here, Tilly, two whole fish from Pa! And I know you don't like cleaning 'em, so I was doing 'em for you." Kipper held up one half-cleaned fish for Tilly to inspect. "Don't smell so bad as usual, neither. Only three days old, Til!"

Tilly's flat face moved, in only a few moments, from anger to bewilderment to a pleased kind of dazed look at having this unpleasant task done for her. "Well, you goes right on with it," she said pleasantly to Kipper. But when she looked at Emily, she gave a disgusted sniff. "Hmmmph! Y'r a mess, ain't you? And that ain't 'zactly the best looking floor job I ever seen."

"Yes, and looky here, Til!" Kipper interrupted.

Then, to Emily's horror, he quickly ground under his heel a bit of fishy newspaper that had fallen to the floor. He lifted it up to reveal an ugly black stain on the linoleum. "She ain't going to be much help 'round *here*," he said almost gleefully. "Look what she missed!"

It was clear that Tilly had seen this whole act from first to last, but she rewarded Kipper with a brazen smile of approval. Then she turned to Emily with a look that could have soured milk. "You gets to do *that* when you comes back. Right now you has to come with me and learn 'bout doing 'round upstairs. You puts y'r stuff 'way, and be quick 'bout it. Us ain't got all day!"

Emily took her brush and pail to a corner of the kitchen and followed Tilly to the door without even a backward look at Kipper. She would not for all the world allow him to see the tears of rage that had sprung to her eyes. She had been taken in by his cheerful look and his good humor, but he was nothing but a liar and a cheat. Such as Tilly was, *she* at least had never really pretended one thing and turned out another.

But what was even deeper than Emily's anger was her despair at losing this one sudden bright hope for a trusted friend. Kipper had joined the ranks of all the other "eyes and ears" of Sugar Hill Hall. Emily was all alone and on her own again, and she felt as if her heart had turned to lead as she trailed after Tilly.

SIX

A Sad Arrival

"You starts with Mrs. Poovey's room, 'cause that's how far I done," Tilly said, stumping into the parlor. "After you sweeps, you makes up a bed, 'cause there's another old one coming in. When you finishes Mrs. Poovey, you moves along to Mr. Bottle and Mr. Dobbs. After that . . ."

As Tilly droned on, Emily's thoughts wandered to the cobwebs and cracked cupids on the ceiling, the tarnished gilt and decaying plaster, the fog creeping past the windows, and the shadows creeping in the parlor. A few of the old people were already stationed in their chairs, staring vacantly ahead and occupied only in waiting for their day to end. Would the time ever come when she would be used to the grim sight of what this room had become? Emily wondered.

Tilly stopped suddenly at the foot of the stairs by the bowl of glistening peppermints. "Well, you already knows what you ain't 'lowed to *touch,* so now you learns where you ain't 'lowed to *go,* and that's one place." She pointed a threatening finger toward a closed door at the far end of the parlor. "It's Mrs. M.'s and Mrs. P.'s dining room, which you was so rudely gawping into after dinner last night. 'Cross from it's Mrs. M.'s room. You *'specially* ain't 'lowed in that one. You gets that?"

"Yes, Tilly," replied Emily, who had as much desire to walk into Mrs. Meeching's room as to enter a pit of snakes. "Am I allowed to go into the ballroom?"

"Ballroom?" said Tilly suspiciously. "*What* ballroom? Ain't no ballroom in *this* house." Then she snickered. "You thinks you come to a castle?"

"There was one when I was here long ago," Emily said, remembering the beautiful ball Aunt and Uncle Twice had held for Mama and Papa in the grand room across from the dining room. "It was right—it was right —but the doors aren't there any more!" Instead of two elegant, gilded doors, Emily had found herself pointing at a blank wall with two dreary pictures hanging from it.

" 'Course not, stoopid! Ain't no ballroom and ain't never been no doors. Y'r brains must be melting 'way from no eating. Anyone what's so picky-picky 'bout the food—" Glaring at Emily, Tilly started up the stairs.

A whole ballroom had disappeared! Stunned by still another question, another mystery, Emily skirted the dangerous peppermint bowl and scurried after Tilly.

"That's Mrs. P.'s room," said Tilly shortly, point-ing to another closed door at the head of the stairs. "Them other doors goes to rooms what ain't occupied. Howsumever, they has to be done up 'cause Mrs. M. shows 'em to perspective customers. Most times y'r aunt 'lows *me* to take care o' *them!*" Tilly added proudly as she turned to start up another stairway.

This one was enclosed and led to an ordinary hall-way also lined with doors. "These ain't yours neither," said Tilly, and started up still another set of stairs. These were very narrow and steep, and Emily's legs ached by the time they arrived at their final destination, a narrow, dark hallway pungent with the smell of dust and old wood peculiar to attics. Outside a half-open door, a broom and mop leaned wearily against a bucket filled with sponges, soap, and rags. A feather duster poked from the bucket like a rooster's tail.

Without knocking, Tilly stumped through the doorway into a room as sparsely furnished and almost as uninviting as Emily's underground cell. Tilly began at once to instruct her on how to clean the room, com-pletely ignoring a little woman in a frayed black wool shawl sitting beside her cot with tiny, bird-sized hands folded quietly in her lap.

Tilly directed a finger at an unmade cot beneath the curtainless window. "First you makes this up f'r the new party coming. Then you sloshes out the wash basin and empties it into the slop jar. When y'r done with that, and done *proper,* you sweeps and dusts." As she spoke, Tilly pulled from a narrow wardrobe two sheets, a worn blanket, and a lumpy pillow and dumped them unceremoniously on the bare mattress.

Emily tried to keep her mind on Tilly's lecture, but it kept wandering to the little old woman, who sat staring out the bare window with empty eyes, as if Emily and Tilly were not even there. This was the tiny, helpless creature who had dared to take the peppermints and been locked in the Remembrance Room. *This* was Mrs. Poovey!

"Emily, ain't you paying no 'tention?" Tilly said crossly.

"Oh yes, Tilly!" Emily quickly picked up a sheet and began clumsily to spread it over the thin hair mattress.

"Hmmmph!" snorted Tilly. "Well, minds you doesn't dawdle." She stumped fiercely from the room, marching back down the stairs with heavy, accusing footsteps.

Emily went on wrestling with the difficult problem of getting the sheet straight on the cot. From time to time she looked shyly over her shoulder at Mrs. Poovey. For all the attention she paid her new young house-keeper, however, Mrs. Poovey might well have been made of wax.

The sheets and blanket finally conquered, Emily went to work trying to put life into the hopeless pillow. *Thump! Thump! Thump!* The sound echoed hollowly against the bare walls and floor. Then the room fell dismally still and silent again. Suppose, Emily wondered, someone spoke directly to Mrs. Poovey. Wouldn't she have to reply? Emily tightened her arms around the pillow and drew a deep breath.

"It—it's a dreadfully foggy day, isn't it?"

Mrs. Poovey didn't even blink.

Emily swallowed hard. "It might be sunnier tomorrow, don't you think?"

If Mrs. Poovey thought that, she gave no sign of it. With a soft sigh, Emily set the pillow on the cot. Now there seemed nothing left to do but go on with her work. She sloshed out the basin and emptied it into the slop jar as Tilly had directed. Then Emily whisked the feather duster over the furnishings and finally began to sweep. She had entirely given up the idea of any conversation with Mrs. Poovey, so to fill the lonely, uncomfortable stillness, she began to hum under her breath. Soon the hum became words.

"London Bridge is falling down," sang Emily. *Whoosh!* went the broom.

"Falling down." *Whoosh!* "Falling down." *Whoosh!*

Suddenly, almost without her knowing it, the words began to change.

"I'll get braver by and by,
By and by, by and by,
All I have to do is try,
My fair lady!

"I will never groan and sigh,
Groan and sigh, groan and sigh,
Mrs. M. can't make me cry,
My fair lady!"

Flustered by what she had done, Emily looked shyly at Mrs. Poovey. Was that a spark in her eyes? Emily's heart leaped. But when she looked again, the spark was gone. In any event, her work in that room was done, so she picked up her broom and mop and bucket. But as she turned to leave, she remembered something else. Despite the way Tilly behaved, Mrs. Poovey was not a chair or a table. She was a person. Emily dropped a curtsy.

"Good day, Mrs. Poovey," she said. "I—I am so pleased to have met you."

But Mrs. Poovey might well have been a chair or a table. She never smiled, or even so much as blinked. Feeling dejected and hopeless, Emily left to find the room described by Tilly as belonging to Mr. Bottle and Mr. Dobbs.

"Mr. Bottle's the one what's got the hankerchee,

case you needs to know," Tilly had said. At the time, Emily had wondered why they couldn't tell her themselves which was which, but after the meeting with Mrs. Poovey, she was beginning to understand. Perhaps though, with two in the room, things might be a little cheerier. Knocking lightly on the open door to announce her presence, she entered.

Wearing patched, thin sweaters, and baggy, threadbare trousers, Mr. Bottle and Mr. Dobbs were seated across from one another on the only two chairs in the room, chairs as straight and stiff as old wooden skeletons.

Mr. Dobbs was snoring, with his chin dropped so far into his hollow chest it seemed intent on working its way to the opposite side. He looked as if he might have fallen asleep over his reading, except that there was nothing to read in his lap unless you considered two gnarled hands to be a book or a newspaper.

The other sound in the room came from Mr. Bottle's thin, red nose. He was, just as Tilly had said, the one with the "hankerchee," a tattered, grey piece of cloth that might have been retired from duty as a cleaning rag because there was so little service left in it. Besides honking into this relic, Mr. Bottle was also studying a small scrap of paper. It was a wrinkled, worn soap wrapper Emily discovered later when she made up his bed, because as soon as she came in, he quickly thrust it under the mattress. It was as if he was actually afraid to be caught reading!

As for any cheer or conversation, Emily soon learned that neither would ever come from *that* room. Mr. Dobbs never did wake up while she was there, and Mr. Bottle only gave muffled replies in one word—or less—from behind his handkerchief, to every attempt at conversation that Emily made. The only sounds that came from the room were whooshing, thumping and swishing, accompanied by the mournful chorus of honking and snoring.

Emily's next sad encounter was with Mrs. Quirk, a lady so tall and thin she seemed like a piece of elastic stretched as far as it could go, then allowed to grow old and brittle in that position so it never could spring back. Emily felt that if Mrs. Quirk swallowed a marble, you would see it travel all the way down her. Moldy bread lumps and fish head stew—no wonder she was wasting away to a shred!

At the moment Emily entered Mrs. Quirk's room, the old lady was seated on her chair waving her fingers about in the most curious way. As soon as she caught sight of Emily, she quickly laid her hands down on her lap, but not before Emily guessed what was happening. She was doing make-believe embroidery, without embroidery thread, needle, or canvas!

Emily, however, could no more start a conversation

with Mrs. Quirk than she could with anyone else. But while she was doing her chores in the sad, silent room, she came to a decision. For the moment, she would forget about Uncle Twice, about the missing ballroom, and all the other mysteries of Sugar Hill Hall. She would devote all her energies toward bringing some happiness, no matter how little, to the pitiful old residents who lived, silent and forgotten, in the upper reaches of this evil mansion. Filled with thoughts of how she might accomplish this, most of them hopeless, she finished her chores and then decided she had better find Tilly for more instructions.

Where was Tilly now? Suddenly the mansion seemed filled with a gloomy hush. Emily set down her bucket and crept quietly down the narrow attic stairs to the floor below. Then she made her way down the hall, room by room, peering through one half open door after another. Some were empty. In others, the old people sat hunched in their chairs, staring and silent like Mrs. Poovey. But Tilly was nowhere to be found. Emily decided finally that she would have to try the floor below. Carefully, she tiptoed down the next flight of steps.

Creak! Pop! Snap! The wooden steps under her feet sounded loud as firecrackers. Mrs. Plumly's room lay almost directly at the foot of the stairs and she wanted to get past it as quickly and quietly as possible. Two more steps to go. One more step to go. No more steps to go—and there was Mrs. Plumly's door. It had been closed when Emily had come up the stairs with Tilly, but now it was a gaping hole! Emily shrivelled back into the safety of the dark stairwell.

Unless she retreated all the way back up the stairs, there was no way to escape going by that door, and she must find Tilly. After waiting a few moments to gather courage, Emily took a deep breath, locked it in her chest, and started out again. She intended to skitter past the doorway like a small insect, not looking through it. But when she reached it, an unbearable curiosity drew her eyes in. She let out her breath with a gasp. There was no one in the room, but what a room it was!

A fire crackled invitingly in a red brick fireplace. Pictures of laughing children danced across wallpaper as sprigged with violets and rosebuds as an old English garden. Crocheted doilies lay on plump chairs and gleaming walnut tables like patches of spring snow. On a tiny mahogany chest of drawers, red-breasted berries nested in a brown china bowl beside a basket spilling over with tangled skeins of yellow wool as soft looking as eiderdown. The room was as cozy as Mrs. Plumly herself. Emily wondered how the thought of it could have made her shiver with fright. Now she could stand and gaze at it for hours. But the gloomy clock in the dining room was already tolling the hour of eleven, and Tilly must be found at once. Quickly, Emily crept past the enticing room.

But as she rounded the balcony, she glanced at the giant mirror that rose up from the first landing, reflecting the whole grim parlor below as clearly as a stereopticon slide. And what she saw brought her to a dead stop. Her heart seemed to jump into her throat and lay there frozen.

Standing before the great oak door of Sugar Hill Hall, just as when Emily had first walked through it, were Mrs. Meeching and Mrs. Plumly. Aunt Twice was in the reflected picture, too, opening the door to four people, two women, a man, and a boy. All four of them were enormously fat. The man had a round, pink face, tremendous jowls as smooth as silk, and tiny, slanted eyes. He was dressed in an expensive black suit with a rich gold chain resting on his stomach. The boy, except for being shorter, seemed to be his exact copy. One of the two women, very much older than the other, though no less fat, was sobbing violently into an impossibly tiny lace handkerchief.

Something in the back of Emily's mind warned her, "If you can see in the mirror, you can also be seen!" Swiftly, she crouched down behind the balcony railing. Then held by a kind of dreadful fascination, she watched the scene being enacted in the room below, revealed in deadly clarity by the mirror.

"So, Mr. and Mrs. Porcus, you have brought us Mrs. Loops," said Mrs. Meeching.

"Yes, Mrs. Meeching, you see we *have* brought her,

just as we said we would," Mr. Porcus said nervously. "Er, just as we said we would," he repeated, looking quite miserable. His arms waved about in a distracted manner as if he were trying to find something to hang on to.

The older woman, who Emily suspected was Mrs. Loops, began to sob again into her small handkerchief.

Mrs. Porcus dropped her first chin consolingly into her second, which in turn dropped into her third. "There, there, dear Aunty," she said, "look at this grand parlor. I'm certain you will be quite comfortable here."

Mr. Porcus looked distinctly *un*comfortable. "Perhaps, Lucine, we should reconsider—"

"Your wife is quite right, Mr. Porcus. Your aunt will indeed be completely comfortable." Emily had trouble recognizing this soothing voice as belonging to Mrs. Meeching, though it did.

Mr. Porcus, who now looked as if he had just floated through a warm oil bath, beamed expansively at Mrs. Meeching. "Well, in that case . . ."

Another heartrending sob from Aunty Porcus (otherwise Mrs. Loops) seemed to have no effect on anybody.

All the while this was going on, the boy was staring at the bowl of peppermints across the parlor, his jaws moving mysteriously inside his fat cheeks as if he were actually chewing one. At last, he began pulling rudely on his mother's coat sleeve and pointing.

"If Albert might be spared one of your delicious peppermints?" inquired Mrs. Porcus of Mrs. Meeching.

"Indeed," said Mrs. Meeching with a shade less soothing oil in her reply. Then the whole joyous party processed across the parlor to the peppermint bowl.

What astonished Emily was that no one in the Porcus family seemed to pay any attention, much less even *see,* the other old people lined up on either side of the parlor. No one, that is, except Aunty, who looked fearfully from left to right, and then threw a fresh wave of useless sobs into her sodden handkerchief.

"We have these for the pleasure of our boarders, although we don't encourage the habit," said Mrs. Meeching as they all stood worshipfully around the glistening bowl. "Bad for the teeth!" she hissed at Albert. Then her lips stretched out like two thin rubber bands in what must have been intended for a smile.

Albert paid no attention to her. The little eyes in his round face stared greedily at the peppermints. All at once his pudgy hand darted out to snatch three of them and stuff them into his mouth. Then, as Mr. and Mrs. Porcus gazed at him fondly, he grabbed a whole handful and stuffed them into his pocket, his face turning scarlet with greed and excitement.

Mrs. Meeching's mouth continued to smile, though the rest of her stiffened perceptibly. But when Albert showed no signs of stopping, her smile grew thinner and thinner, and finally disappeared altogether.

"Mrs. Luccock!" she snapped. "You may now show Mrs. Loops to her room!" Then she firmly steered the remaining Porcus family, with peppermint-flavored Albert trotting happily beside them, through the front door. Mr. and Mrs. Porcus, quite unaware of the sudden frost in the air, seemed so relieved to have gotten rid of Aunty that they offered no resistance at all.

Emily remained hidden until Mrs. Meeching returned to her room and Aunt Twice, accompanied by Mrs. Plumly, had led the sobbing Mrs. Loops up the stairs. Too shaken now to continue her search for Tilly, Emily slipped noiselessly down the stairs and made her way to the kitchen. One person she did not want to see there when she arrived was Kipper, but she needn't have worried about that. When she arrived, the kitchen was empty. A few fish scales still clinging damply to the grey sink were the only signs that the fishmonger's boy had even been there.

SEVEN

Peppermint Peril

It was two days later when Tilly announced that she was to be taken shopping with Mrs. Meeching. "Y'r aunt's to be busy baking cakes, so I gets to help Mrs. Meeching buy the groceries," said Tilly proudly. She sounded as if she were actually going to have her opinion sought in selecting strawberries out of season, the limes and the lettuces, instead of merely going along to serve as a beast of burden, weighted down with Mrs. Meeching's packages.

"And since I hasn't the time to dust the parlor"— Tilly was all importance this morning—"*you* gets to do it today, Emily." To Tilly, dusting the parlor was clearly an honor not to be bestowed on anyone else except in cases of direst emergency, or as in the present instance, simply if something better came along. She handed Emily a rag and flounced off to prepare herself for her big excursion, leaving Emily alone in the parlor.

Well, not quite alone, because, of course, there were some of the old people in the room as well. From having cleaned their rooms, Emily could now attach names to several of the sad, wrinkled faces. Mr. Bottle and his handkerchief were in the parlor. So was Mr. Popple with the ears so big and thin you could see light through them. Also present was Mrs. Biggs, who still wore spectacles stiff as cat's whiskers perched on her nose, even though the glass in them had long since been lost—or stolen.

But for all useful purposes, such as conversation or company, Emily *was* alone. And though Tilly might have numbered dusting the parlor with other treasured gifts from her gracious benefactors, Emily didn't see it at all in the same light. She did not like being in the parlor on her own and wanted to get the chore done as quickly as possible.

It was so very quiet in the room. So very dim. So very frightening to be stared at by unseeing faces and to be in the presence of two doors, closed like lids over baleful eyes, doors that could spring open at any moment. Except for an occasional honk from Mr. Bottle, who sat hunched in a chair to one side of Mrs. Meeching's closed door, the parlor remained deadly silent as Emily's dust rag raced over the tables.

She had gone no more than halfway around the room when suddenly Mrs. Meeching's door swung open. Emily gasped, her hand frozen in midair, as Mrs. Meeching appeared dressed for shopping in a black coat and hat that made her look strangely like a snake attempting to masquerade as a lady. She hurried silently across the parlor and climbed the stairs toward Mrs. Plumly's room, but in her hurry, she had left behind an *open door!* Through it Emily could see a blood-red carpet, heavy, blood-red velvet draperies shrouding the windows, and furniture that gave the impression of being dark, oversized headstones.

Then all at once, the silent parlor was shattered with an explosion of sound. *Ker! Ker! Choo!* It was Mr. Bottle sneezing. He dove into the pocket of his sweater to retrieve the rag that passed for his handkerchief. And *Plop!* Along with the handkerchief, a peppermint flew right out of the pocket and fell to the floor. But instead of stopping where it fell, it went rolling. And rolling. And rolling. It did not stop until it reached the dead center of Mrs. Meeching's carpet where it lay blinking like a knowing, wicked red-and-white eyeball. "Come and get me," it taunted, "anyone who dares!"

Thoughts, each one more chilling than the one that came before it, darted through Emily's head. Mr. Bottle clearly had not seen or heard the peppermint fall. She could tell him about it, and no doubt have a Mr. Bottle instantly dead with fright lying on the parlor floor. If Mrs. Meeching saw the peppermint upon her return, she would immediately suspect one of the old people, and the most likely culprit would be Mr. Bottle, since he was nearest the door. There was only one thing to be done, and that was for Emily to go for the peppermint.

Dropping the rag on the nearest table, she flew swiftly to the open door. Then with her breath as solid in her throat as a lump of moldy bread, she tiptoed into the dreaded room. And then she froze. In that deathly silent parlor, *any* sound could be heard, but most especially the sound of *footsteps*. Mrs. Meeching, having completed her business with Mrs. Plumly, was on her way back to her room!

There was another door in that room, closed, and two large wardrobes, also with doors closed. But it was already firmly implanted in Emily's mind that closed doors at Sugar Hill Hall were to be avoided like the plague. Besides, with Mrs. Meeching's breath practically felt in the room, there was no time to play musical doors. And then she saw the hiding place that offered her one slim hope. Scooping up the peppermint, she slipped behind the blood-red velvet folds of the draperies.

It was, however, a surprisingly noisy, rough Mrs. Meeching that finally entered the room. *Clash! Crash! Bang!* Emily heard what sounded like logs tumbling into the fireplace. And there was a voice that came with them.

"Ouch! Well, if that ain't the catfish's whiskers, as Pa always says. A blamed splinter! Ouch! Ouch!" The voice belonged to the fishmonger's son.

Good, thought Emily, serves him right! But she was still frightened. This was not Mrs. Meeching, but how much better was Kipper? After the way he had behaved in the kitchen with Tilly, think how he would relish turning Emily over to Mrs. Meeching! If only he would hurry with his logs and leave so Emily could escape to the parlor. But he was still dawdling with them when Mrs. Meeching returned.

"How dare you enter my room without permission!" she hissed at him in a voice stiff with rage.

"Well, the door was open, mum, 'n' I wanted to get the logs built so's you could have a nice fire aroaring 'fore you got back." Kipper was using the same brand of oil he had applied to Tilly.

"Oh, I suppose that's all right. But see you don't do it again."

"'Oh no, mum!" said Kipper earnestly.

For a few moments there was only the sound of wood being knocked against wood, and a drawer sliding open and shut. Then suddenly Mrs. Meeching said sharply, "What was that?"

"What was what, mum?"

"That sound. I heard something drop."

Something had indeed dropped—the peppermint from Emily's hand! It fell right by her feet, but unfortunately just beyond the edge of the velvet drapery for the whole room to see, if it looked in the right place.

"I didn't hear anything, mum," said Kipper brightly. "Expect it were a bit o' wood falling."

"Nonsense! I heard *something.*" Suspicion oozed from every letter of the word.

Then logs clattered noisily in the fireplace, and Mrs. Meeching hissed her displeasure.

"Sorry 'bout that, mum," Kipper piped up.

"Oh, never mind!" snarled Mrs. Meeching. "But as long as I must put up with this, there *are* a few words I've been meaning to have with you." She lowered her voice. "Have you met the orphan brat that's come here to live?"

"Yes, mum. I met the skinny little thing in the kitchen th'other day. Ain't worth much, I'd say."

"Quite right, Kipper! I'm only keeping her here out of the kindness of my heart—to please Mrs. Luccock. But I'm afraid Emily isn't to be trusted. Do you understand my meaning?"

"Oh *yes,* mum!" said Kipper soulfully.

"Well—" There was a long pause filled with meaning. "What I want you to do is keep an eye on her whenever you're here. Report to me if you catch her doing anything—*suspicious.* Snooping about, as it were. If you do, there's a packet of peppermints in it for you!"

"Yum! Yum!" said Kipper.

"Ahhh! I see you'd like that, eh?"

"Yum! Yum!"

"That's right, rub your stomach! Well, come to me with a report, and you shall have one."

"Oh *thank you,* mum! Yum! Yum!"

"Well, that's settled then. Now, aren't you finished with that fireplace yet?"

"I'm not near done yet, mum. But you ain't got any cause to worry. I'll just finish up and close the door tight shut when I go."

"You must do more than that, Kipper. You must fetch Mrs. Plumly to lock up."

"Yes, mum, I'll do that all right. Oh yes, mum."

"That's a very good boy." Kipper's oily performance was clearly having its effect on Mrs. Meeching. "Well then, I shall now leave, and—don't forget the packet of peppermints!"

"Oh *no,* mum! I won't forget. Yum! Yum!"

That slimy, slimy fishmonger's boy! That horrible, treacherous Mrs. Meeching! Behind the velvet drapery, Emily was a seething mixture of horror and terror and rage.

A few moments passed, and then with a start, she realized that the room had suddenly become very quiet. Had Kipper already gone for Mrs. Plumly? With one trembling finger, Emily pushed the red velvet aside an inch. And found herself staring straight into a pair of scowling blue eyes!

"See here, *ain't* you got more sense 'n to come nosing 'round in the snake pit? *Ain't* you 'ware that the snake lady eats folks five times your size for *breakfast?* And lastest, but far and 'way not the leastest, seems to me you dropped something." Kipper opened up a stern hand to reveal the offending peppermint. "Here, Emily! Yum! Yum!"

EIGHT

Fish Syrup

"Now, Miss Emily, best we get a few things straightened out 'fore you end up being the main course front o' the snake lady at her nextest meal!" Kipper strode purposefully into the cellar laundry room, glaring at Emily. He had ordered her to wait there for him while he finished his business with Mrs. Plumly. "First, howsumever, best you tell me exactly what you was doing snooping 'bout in that room, and then you can tell me what kind o' foolishness you was up to stealing a peppermint!"

"I—I—I—" stammered Emily. Then suddenly this was all too much for her, and she ended up doing what she had vowed she would not do. She burst into tears.

The look in Kipper's eyes instantly softened. "Come on now, don't cry. I'm sorry, truly I am. I shouldn't o' spoken to you so cross after the horrors you just been through. No matter what you done, you most likely been punished 'nough already."

"But I didn't do *anything!*" sobbed Emily. "I mean, not what you think. I wasn't snooping, and I didn't steal a peppermint. Someone else dropped—I—I mean, it just fell from somewhere, and I ran in to get it."

"Fell from somewhere? From *heaven* I 'spect! Well, I should o' guessed!" Kipper slapped his forehead. "You was on a rescue mission, but you don't want to tell me for what party 'cause you still ain't certain 'bout my credentuals. Well, can't say I blame you any after my performance in the kitchen for old Tilly."

"Performance?" asked Emily.

Kipper grinned wryly. "That's what it were, Emily, no more 'n just a performance. Didn't have time to explain 'bout it 'fore I done it and haven't found time to explain 'bout it afterwards. But I done it so's Tilly wouldn't think you and me was getting too friendly right off. You got to work Tilly just right, remembering that she ain't got any Aunt Twice to care for her, nor any Pa either, and she goes pea green over anyone liking anyone else what ain't Tilly. Now, does that explain why I done what I done?"

Emily nodded, unable to speak. She knew now that she had found a friend after all, and her feet felt as if they were floating six inches above the ground.

"Well then," said Kipper, "would you like to explain further why *you* done what *you* done? Meaning, who you're aiming to pertect?"

"It—it was Mr. Bottle," Emily said. "He pulled out his handkerchief and out popped the peppermint onto the floor. It rolled into Mrs. Meeching's room, and I went after it."

"So it were Mr. Bottle!" exclaimed Kipper. "Well, I'll be a pickled perch, as Pa always says."

"I couldn't let Mrs. Meeching find the peppermint and blame poor Mr. Bottle for stealing it," Emily said. "It might have killed him dead away!"

"Might have at that," said Kipper. "What you done was a kind, brave thing, Emily, but you shouldn't o' had to do it." His face flushed with anger. "Blamed peppermints! Don't know why the snake lady keeps 'em 'round except for meanness, or to act as an evil spell. That's what they are, Emily! No reason why she can't 'low them poor old ones a taste or two now and then. She says it ruints their choppers. Ha! Most o' them ain't *got* choppers excepting the ones they put by their beds at night. And as for Tilly—"

"What about Tilly?" Emily asked.

"Well, Tilly's not a hardhearted girl, nor anything like that, but—" Kipper hesitated, and then began to sing softly still another made-up verse to "London Bridge,"

"Tilly tells for peppermints,
Peppermints, peppermints,
Tilly tells for peppermints,
Best be careful!"

"O' course," he added quickly, "ain't right to be too hard on her, Emily. She don't know any better, and the snake lady is most all the family she knows. But you best be careful 'round her, anyways. You best be careful 'bout *everything*. It ain't just a shrimp nor a sardine what swims into a net, as Pa always says. But speaking o' being careful, what are we to do 'bout this?" Kipper dipped into his pocket and brought out the peppermint that had been the cause of so much peril for Emily.

She shuddered at the sight of it. "What if Mr. Bottle goes to look for it and can't find it? Won't he die of fright all the same?"

"Them old folks' memories ain't too good," Kipper said. "I expect he might just think he's et it already and forgot when."

"Then *you* eat it," said Emily.

"Not *me!*" Kipper grinned ruefully. "If you got to know the truth, peppermints give me the pip."

Emily giggled.

"Say, I know what I'll do with the peppermint!" Kipper exclaimed. He shoved it back into his pocket. "I'll give it to one o' the little water rats, which is what Pa calls the urchins what live 'round the wharf. I'll give it to Little Shrimper what carries water for him when I'm not 'round. But look, I best be going now. I ain't expected to be here lest I'm doing a chore."

"Will—will I see you soon again?" Emily asked.

"Not too soon, I'm 'fraid. Now you're here, I ain't going to be given as much work to do."

"Oh, I'm sorry, Kipper!" Emily cried.

"Now, ain't your fault you come free," Kipper said cheerfully. "Anyways, I'm building up a delivery business. I got two reg'lar customers now, and I'll get more. So don't you worry any 'bout it. Just mind and *be careful!* With that warning, and a warm smile, Kipper left, and Emily was alone again.

§♠

It turned out to be five whole long dreary days before Kipper returned to the mansion. In the meantime, Emily made not one step of progress toward helping the old people. She began to wonder if they were all too sunk in despair and fearful old age *ever* to be helped. As for solving any of the mysteries, she was no further along than when she had first arrived. The only happy spot in her life was a conversation she had had with Aunt Twice about Mama and Papa, even though it was cut short by the arrival of Tilly again wanting to talk about *her* departed ma and pa.

As for the food, Emily still could not eat more than

a few bites of the soup (or gruel, or stew, depending on the time of day), and none of the bread, so she was growing weaker and weaker. As a result, her work, instead of getting better, was growing worse. This meant that Tilly was having to work harder, and so despite her own healthy appetite, was getting tireder and tireder, and as a result, crosser and crosser. She grumbled continuously about the quality of Emily's work and constantly referred to "them good ol' days" when Kipper was hired to help with the chores.

It was early one afternoon, and Emily was at work in the laundry room. Steam poured from large tin wash boilers on the stove. Water drizzled down stone walls already blackened and mildewed by ten thousand earlier laundries. Baskets were heaped with mountains of dirty linens that seemed to Emily to grow taller and taller instead of shorter and shorter as she washed.

She was kneeling on the cold, damp stone floor before an iron wash tub, trying to rub the spots from a very dirty linen sheet. Her knuckles scraped painfully on the wicked zinc crimps of the washboard, and tears were again perilously close to spilling down her cheeks. Tilly had left her with a severe warning that she had better have at least *one* thing properly washed, and Emily was certain that Tilly would return long before any spots or stains had departed.

Suddenly, Emily heard a voice over the sound of the wash bubbling gloomily on the stove.

"Ain't much fun down on your knees,
On your knees, on your knees,
I will help you, if you please,
My fair lady!"

"Kipper!"

"None other! See here, you look 'bout done in. And I meant the words in the song. How 'bout letting me take a turn at that?" As he was talking, Kipper was already peeling off his jacket and rolling up his shirtsleeves.

"No!" Emily shook her head hard. "It wouldn't be fair."

"What wouldn't be fair 'bout it?"

"You wouldn't be paid for it as you were before."

Kipper shrugged. "Don't matter. Pa says you don't need to be paid for every least thing you do, not in money, anyways. He says living's a payment for breathing, and a smile's a payment for a good turn. A smile's all I need, Emily."

Emily obliged him with one, but then looked fearfully over her shoulder. "What about Tilly?"

"Remember what I said 'bout working Tilly just right?" Kipper grinned. "Well, my performance worked! She knows she ain't got anything to worry 'bout where you and me is concerned. When I told her I'd come to help with the laundry *free*, she looked pleased as pleased can be. Old Til ain't ever minded anyone helping with the chores 'round Sugar Hill Hall what I can recollect. So move on over and let me at the washboard!"

Kipper dipped his strong, freckled arms into the tub and went after the dirty linen as if he were attacking a sea serpent. Emily couldn't believe how quickly the stubborn spots vanished.

"Say," he said, examining her critically over the washboard, "ain't you got more'n that to wear? Last two times I seen you, you been in the same garment. I know it ain't polite to say so, Emily, but that dress looks 'bout ready to be a soot rag."

"Oh, I had another dress, but—but . . ." Emily's voice faded, "I gave it to Tilly."

"Gave it to *Tilly!*" Kipper exploded. "Whatever for? Tilly couldn't get anything o' *yours* over her head."

"She thought it was pretty," Emily said, remembering the endless hour she had spent going over the "pretty things" in her travelling bag with Tilly. "So I just gave it to her."

"More'n likely she just took it!" said Kipper. "Poor old Til ain't ever had anything pretty. Anyways," he shook his head, "I expect the other dress ain't any more useful than the one you got on."

"It won't be for long," Emily said quickly. "I have two trunks coming filled with clothes."

"Well, I hope it don't take too long for 'em to get here, else your dress will fall right off o' you." Kipper appraised Emily's appearance again and sighed. "You know something? You're the skinniest person I ever did see. And getting skinnier all the time. Ain't you eating any o' that delicious soup and bread pervided by the management?" He grinned wryly.

"I try," Emily said. "I think I'm hungry, but when I get to the table and see the food, I can't eat it."

"And to think o' all them good things your aunt fixes for the snake lady!" Kipper said grimly. "Enough to feed a dozen and lots to spare too. Beats me what they do with it all."

"Do you wonder about that too?" Emily looked over her shoulder again and dropped her voice. "Oh, Kipper, there are so many mysteries about Sugar Hill Hall. So many questions! A second one is about Mrs. Plumly. Why should anyone who appears to be so nice be friends with Mrs. Meeching?"

Kipper shook his head. "Never have figured that one out either."

"And—and there's the ballroom too," Emily said. "What ballroom?"

"There, you see!" Emily exclaimed softly. "Tilly didn't know about it—she said I was stupid—and now you don't know about it either. But there *is* a ballroom, Kipper, right across from the dining room, even though there aren't any doors."

"You know something, Emily," Kipper said thoughtfully, "I ain't of the mind that you're stupid at all. I think maybe you're right 'bout some kind o' room there. You can tell it outside from the shape o' the mansion, excepting there ain't any windows. I used to wonder 'bout it. Say!" He looked curiously at Emily. "How come you know so much 'bout a room there?"

"Because I was here when I was a little girl."

Kipper's eyes widened. *"Here?"*

"Yes! And there was a huge ballroom with two big gold doors right where I said. I was here with Mama and Papa, and a big ball was given for them by Aunt Twice and Uncle Twice. Oh!" Emily gasped and threw a hand to her mouth.

"What's wrong?" Kipper asked anxiously.

Emily began to tremble. "I—I promised Aunt Twice I would never say his name aloud. She told me I was to think of him as—as *dead!*"

"Well, I ain't ever heard of any Uncle Twice alive *or* dead," Kipper said. "But now I know 'bout him, ain't any more cause for you not to tell me all you know, Emily."

This couldn't be denied, so she poured out the whole conversation she had had with her aunt on the first night at Sugar Hill Hall, including the information that Aunt Twice was being held prisoner there to protect someone's life.

"Wheeoo!" Kipper whistled softly when she had finished. "I always suspicioned there was some kind o' hokus-pokus 'bout this place, and your aunt acting scairt out o' her wits and all that, but never so much as that,

Emily. You know something? I wonder if it's your *uncle's* life she's pertecting."

"That's what *I* thought," Emily told him. "But what if it isn't? What if it's someone else's life? Supposing Uncle Twice has become a—a wicked man, and supposing Aunt Twice is protecting someone from *him*?"

"That's lots o' supposing you're doing," Kipper said. "Right now we ain't got proof o' anything."

"How do we get proof?" Emily asked.

"Don't rightly know. All I *do* know is we got to keep our wits sharp, our eyes open, and our mouths shut, excepting to each other. Agreed?"

Emily nodded. "Agreed!"

"But for now," Kipper went on, "lest you waste 'way to a minnow, as Pa always says, first thing you got to do is increase your appetite so's you *can* eat the soup and the bread. If only you could have some o' Pa's fish syrup. That'd build up your appetite so's you could eat just 'bout anything."

"Fish syrup?" It sounded worse to Emily than all the pills and potions she had ever had to choke down in her life.

Kipper laughed aloud. "What a face! It don't taste all that bad!" Still chuckling, he returned to scrubbing. But suddenly he sat back on his heels and slapped his leg with a loud, wet smack. "Dingus, Emily, I'm going to bring you some o' that syrup! Pa'll let me have all I want. I know he will for that *poor little mite,* which is what he's calling you now. You can hide it in your room, and not the snake lady, nor Tilly, nor anybody else need know 'bout it. Will you take it if I bring it?"

"What if I can't keep it down?" Emily remembered all too well her earlier experiences along this line.

"Oh, you won't have any trouble," Kipper said. "Fish syrup goes down smooth and easy. Ain't anybody I ever knowed of giving it back once it slid past their gullet. Will you try it?"

Emily hesitated a moment, but finally nodded.

Kipper beamed. "You won't be sorry. You'll see. Pa'll be pleased. Soon you'll be eating everything. Then when you—"

As Kipper talked, Emily's mind began to wander. It wandered right out of the laundry room, up the stairs and through the kitchen, past the dining room and the parlor, and on up the stairs to the upper reaches of Sugar Hill Hall. There it finally stopped as she thought, if there was something that could help *her* appetite, couldn't it also help the appetites of the old people? *Fish syrup.* It certainly didn't sound like something she would have chosen for a plan to help them, considering how she herself felt about potions and pills. But it had possibilities. And it was a beginning. *Fish syrup.* Well?

"Emily? Emily! Ain't you been listening to a word I said?"

"Kipper," Emily's voice came from far away, "how

many bottles of fish syrup will your Pa let you bring?"

"How many bottles?" Kipper looked puzzled. "As many as you like, but how many bottles can a tadpole your size put away?"

"Not *me*, silly!" exclaimed Emily. "The *old people!* If it can improve my appetite, it ought to improve theirs, too."

"No doubt, 'cause it improves *everybody's*. But who would give it to them, and how?"

"Me," replied Emily. "And—and I could take it around to them in my cleaning bucket."

Kipper shook his head so violently the red curls danced onto his forehead. "Too dangerous. I ain't 'bout to 'low that."

"Oh, Kipper, I'm certain I could do it safely. No one would ever find out."

"We-e-ell . . ." Kipper scratched one ear with a soapy finger.

"Please, Kipper. Say you'll bring it."

"We-e-ell . . ." Kipper scratched the other ear. "Don't know how Pa'll take to it, you taking such chances."

"Please!" Emily pleaded. "I'll be *so* careful. I promise!"

"We-e-ell," said Kipper. And with no more ears left to scratch, he finally agreed to bring enough fish syrup for everyone.

NINE

An Unexpected Invitation

Emily pushed open the kitchen door and peered stealthily across the dining room. *Tock! Tock! Tock!* Only the face of the grandfather clock, tolling its mournful tale, was there to look down on her. Still, she hesitated. She had long since begun to wish that Kipper had gone on scratching his ears until he had concluded that she could not take, that he would not *allow* her to take, the fish syrup around to all the old people. Having an exciting idea when talking with Kipper in the comparative safety of the laundry room was one thing, but carrying it out all on her own in the shadows of Sugar Hill Hall was another. She could not, however, stand there waiting forever.

Her heart lodged somewhere near her throat, she ran on tiptoes across the dining room. Then she peeked cautiously into the parlor. Even with the syrup bottle well hidden under the rags in her bucket, she was relieved to find no one there but a few old people, staring across the room with unseeing eyes. She scurried past the peppermints and started up the stairs. She had gone no more than three steps, however, when she heard the sound of heavy boots stumping down to the landing. She looked up with a start, expecting to see Tilly.

Instead she saw a man wearing an extraordinarily untidy sea captain's uniform coming directly toward her. His face had not had the attention of a razor in some days and was as ugly a face as Emily had ever seen. Through a mat of coarse stubble, a bulbous nose, decorated by a wart large and black as a fly, swelled out over thick, rubbery lips. A scarlet gash seared one cheek from chin to ear.

Emily stared at the sea captain with fixed eyes, and he stared back. She felt as if she was suddenly covered with a sheet of ice. Who was this ugly horror of a man? What was he doing at Sugar Hill Hall? What might he do to *her* right then? His eyes seemed to drill a hole right through the bucket to the bottle of fish syrup.

But whatever his business there, it had nothing to do with Emily. He simply brushed right past her with only a twitch of a squinted, bloodshot eye. The grandfather clock must have tocked away a whole minute before Emily was able to move again. Still trembling, she hurried on up the stairs. With eyes intently fastened on her feet lest she stumble and drop the bucket, she was all the way to the head of the stairs before she saw Mrs. Plumly standing in her doorway, watching.

"Oh!" Emily gasped.

"My dear child!" exclaimed Mrs. Plumly. It was the first time Emily had ever heard her voice, and it was sweet and musical, matching Mrs. Plumly perfectly. "I'm so sorry. Did I frighten you?"

"N-no," stammered Emily. "I—I was only startled."

"But you do look so pale, my dear. Did something else alarm you?" Mrs. Plumly looked alarmed herself. Her round face was puckered up into a whole map of pink wrinkles.

Emily nodded. "A—a sea captain, coming down the stairs. He—he was ugly and horrible-looking."

"Sea captain? Ugly?" Mrs. Plumly looked puzzled. Then suddenly her eyebrows raised. "Ah! I think I know the person you mean. Now, what could *he* be doing prowling about Sugar Hill Hall? We can't have this. I must speak to Mrs. Meeching about it. But not yet, child. I—I've been wanting so much to speak with you. Wait!" Mrs. Plumly held up a warning finger, then tiptoed to the bannister and looked into the mirror that reflected the parlor below.

Quickly, she tiptoed back and beckoned Emily into her room. "Come! It's safe now. Come into my room, dear child."

Emily was so surprised and overwhelmed by this unexpected invitation that she could hardly put one foot before the other. As soon as she entered the cozy room, Mrs. Plumly swiftly closed the door behind her.

"Oh, my dear child, I have wanted so much to

speak with you. I have been so lonely for the sound of a young voice. As you can see, all I have now is my pictures and my memories." She looked sadly toward all the photographs on the walls. "But please, please do sit down for just a moment."

Still unable to believe that she was actually in this delightful room with Mrs. Plumly, Emily set down her bucket and seated herself on a small walnut rocker beside the fireplace. A teakettle sang softly over the glowing coals, and before it a silver dish of tiny cakes lay temptingly on a low table.

Mrs. Plumly settled down soft as a Christmas pudding into a pale green velvet armchair across the table. "Now, please do help yourself to some cakes," she said in her melodious voice, smiling at Emily.

Emily could easily have taken a handful of the luscious little cakes. She felt so empty. The fish syrup had gone down smoothly, just as Kipper predicted it would, but she had not been taking it long enough yet for it to have had much effect when she faced the morning menu of tasteless gruel. Good manners, however, stood in the way of present hunger.

"Thank you very much, Mrs. Plumly," she said, and took one small cherry cream tart.

"Oh my sweet child," Mrs. Plumly said quickly, "please have another. You must be so hungry. And please, too, won't you call me Aunty Plum when we are alone together? It would mean such a great deal to me."

"Y-y-yes, Aunty—Aunty Plum," said Emily shyly.

"That's so much better!" Mrs. Plumly smiled again. Then her smile faded suddenly. She jumped up from her chair and ran to the door, her yellow flowered skirt whispering anxiously across the floor. She stood for a few moments with her ear pressed against the door before returning to collapse into her seat. Her face was stiff with fear.

"It's all right, child," she said, breathing heavily. "There's no one there. I didn't mean to alarm you."

"Oh Aunty Plum, are you—are you—" Emily could not go on.

"Speak, child," said Mrs. Plumly urgently. "What is it you wish to say?"

"Aunty Plum, are you—are you a prisoner of Sugar Hill Hall, too, like—like Aunt Twice?"

Mrs. Plumly nodded stiffly. "Yes, dear, I too am a prisoner." Her eyes swam in tears. "Only I, thanks be to someone's kindness, am more fortunate than the other sad inmates of this mansion."

Thanks be to someone's kindness! Emily drew in a sharp breath. "Aunty Plum, are *you* the one whose very life depends on—on Aunt Twice?" She had blurted it out before she could stop herself.

Mrs. Plumly looked as if she had turned to stone. "Did—did your Aunt Twice mention any name?"

"N-n-no," stammered Emily, thoroughly frightened. "She would not tell me."

Mrs. Plumly's soft grey eyes now burned with a terrible fear. "Please, please, child, ask no more questions of your aunt, or of me." She looked over her shoulder with a deep shudder. "The walls here have eyes and ears!"

The eyes and ears of Sugar Hill Hall—again! Whose? thought Emily, trembling.

"Now I'm afraid you must leave, my dear Emily," Mrs. Plumly said, finally collecting herself. "I've kept you here too long already. But before you go, please do promise two things. One is that you will be very, very careful. And the other is that you will return again some time to see me."

"I promise both," Emily said earnestly, and then they parted.

But as she carried her bucket up the stairs, more questions plummeted through her mind. There was one question, however, she no longer needed to ask anyone. For Emily now knew as surely as she knew how night followed day that Mrs. Plumly *was* the one Aunt Twice was protecting! But that answer only served to open up a new question—*why?*

༄

Kipper marched into the cellar laundry room carrying two paper sacks in his hands. He set them both down carefully on the stone floor and began to unwrap his green-and-white-striped muffler. "Well, did you do it?" His eyes were bluer than ever with suppressed excitement.

"I *did!*" Emily smiled up at him from over her washboard.

"Dingus, Emily! Did you have any trouble? I mean, you didn't get seen nor anything?" As he talked, Kipper was already rolling up his sleeves, prepared to help with the wash. He dropped to his knees before a second tub Tilly had thoughtfully placed there as soon as she learned he was willing to offer his services free of charge.

"Well—" Emily said. She hardly knew where to begin. "Oh, Kipper, I have so much to tell you!"

"Then best start telling," said Kipper with a cheerful grin.

But before Emily had finished her story, the grin had long since faded and been replaced by a thoughtful, somber expression. "Sounds mighty like you're right 'bout Mrs. Plumly being the one your aunt is pertecting," he said. "And if that's so, it makes for lots more questions."

"I know," Emily said. "And I don't—I don't like any of them, Kipper!" Her voice broke.

"Now, see here, don't you go doing any more o' them supposings 'bout your Uncle Twice, Emily. Ain't anything definite 'bout anything. Come now," he said with a reassuring bob of his head, "tell me more 'bout that sea cap'n. You say he had a nasty wart on top o' his nose and a red cut going all the way from his chin to his ear?"

Emily nodded.

"Well, you know if that ain't a exact description o' Cap'n Scurlock, I'll eat a live eel, as Pa always says."

"Do you mean you know him?" Emily asked.

"Don't know him personal," Kipper replied. "Just know he's a mighty nasty indiwidual, him and all his wicked crew. Mrs. Plumly's right not to want the likes o' him prowling 'round Sugar Hill Hall. Wonder what he was up to. I ain't seen him but once or twice inside here as I can recollect, and then only having a word with the snake lady at the front door. But see here, we never got 'round to talking 'bout the fish syrup. You never did tell Mrs. Plumly 'bout it, did you?" he asked anxiously.

Emily shook her head.

"Good! Best not tell anyone 'bout it, Emily. Not *anyone!*"

"I won't," Emily promised. "I don't think we should, either."

"But you never did say," Kipper continued, "do the old ones take to the fish syrup?"

"Oh yes!" cried Emily. "They take it like lambs, the ones I can give it to without being seen. But, Kipper, they just open their mouths for the syrup, like babies who have grown very old without ever learning to speak or smile. I wonder now if I'll ever be able to help them."

"But ain't anybody's appetite growing any bigger?" Kipper asked.

"Well, some of them *do* finish their soup now, as I'm beginning to, but they won't touch the bread. Until they do, you know Mrs. Meeching won't get them any fresh."

"Give 'em time," said Kipper. "Anyways, I brung you some more syrup."

"Oh good!" Emily clapped her hands together. "I doubt there's a spoonful left in the bottle. Is it in those bags you brought?"

"It's in one o' them," Kipper replied carelessly. "How 'bout you going over to find out what's in the other?"

Emily looked at him curiously, but he suddenly became very intent on scrubbing a piece of linen on his washboard. She quickly wiped her hands on her bedraggled dress and ran over to the sacks. Dropping to her knees, she carefully opened one sack and lifted out three large brown bottles of fish syrup. But when she started to open the second sack, she heard an odd little squeak coming from deep inside it. She looked at Kipper with surprise, looked inside the sack, and then threw her hands to her mouth.

"Oh! Oh! Oh! A kitten! A little calico kitten!

Where did it come from? And who is it for?"

"Come from Pa's and my Blackie," said Kipper, beaming from ear to ear. "And it's for you! I been busting to tell you. I was afraid it'd wake up and spoil my surprise."

"A kitten!" breathed Emily rapturously, lifting it carefully from the sack. "But where will I keep it, and how will I feed it?"

"Feeding's easy, what with Pa's fish business," Kipper replied. "As for keeping it, well, I guess as how Pa and me'll have to keep it. But I'll bring it to you from time to time so's you can play with it, Emily."

Emily set the kitten gently down on the floor. Just as she did, a drop of water flew out from Kipper's tub and splashed onto its nose. Startled, the kitten arched its back and pranced across the floor. Emily giggled. Then she held out her hand, and the kitten came to sniff at it. Assured of its safety, the kitten suddenly rolled over on its back so that nothing could be seen but its soft white chest, which looked to Emily exactly like Mama's lambswool powder puff that she had once loved to play with.

"Oh, Kipper," she breathed, "if only I could keep it just for tonight. Could I?"

" 'Fraid not, Emily." Kipper shook his head firmly. "Too much danger. Anyways, where'd you keep it?"

Emily thought a moment. "There's a tiny room up from mine that's not locked because there's nothing in it. Tilly never has a need to go in there, and neither does Aunt Twice."

"We-e-ell . . ."

"Please, Kipper! Only for one night. I won't ask for more."

"But I ain't coming back tomorrow, Emily. I ain't going to be here 'til the day after to deliver the fish."

"Two nights aren't any more dangerous than one. Please say you'll leave it!" Emily pleaded.

"Well," Kipper said uncertainly, "I *guess* it would be all right. I've brought enough fish, and a bit o' milk. But no more than two nights, now!"

"Oh, Kipper!" Emily whispered, stroking the kitten's velvety ears. "If only I could take it around for the old people to see."

Kipper's head jerked up so suddenly he almost toppled over. "Oh no!" he said sternly. "Oh no, Miss Emily, none o' that! I ain't going to have anything left but grey hair time you get through with all your dangerous notions. There's to be no taking the kitten out o' this cellar!"

"But I take the fish syrup around," said Emily. "Why is it that I can take the fish syrup if I can't take the kitten?"

" 'Cause," said Kipper fiercely, "fish syrup don't mew, Emily!"

"Oh!" said Emily meekly.

TEN

Mrs. Poovey and Mrs. Loops

Slowly.

   Slowly.

      Slowly.

Emily crept up the stairs. She was clutching her bucket so tightly her hand ached. Deep inside the bucket, curled up in a nest of sponges and rags and covered with torn scraps of muslin, lay the kitten. Its tiny stomach swelled with two whole saucers of milk, it was now soundly, and safely, asleep.

But what if it should awaken? What if Emily should run into the ugly Captain Scurlock again, or even Mrs. Plumly, who should no more know about the kitten than the fish syrup? Or, horror of horrors, what if Emily should run into Mrs. Meeching herself? Despite all these possible dangers, however, and despite the solemn warning of the grandfather clock in the dining room, Emily's footsteps continued on their dangerous journey, almost as if they had a mind of their own.

Slowly.

    Slowly.

        Slowly.

By the time she crept from the dark, narrow stairwell that led to the attic, her legs felt ready to buckle under her. And the hand that reached out to tap on Mrs. Poovey's and Mrs. Loops's door was cold as the underground stones of Sugar Hill Hall. But she was safe! Now all that remained was to discover if bringing the kitten was worth the terrible risk.

She stood outside the door, knowing that no one would answer her knock, whether the room was empty or not. But she would never march into one of the old people's rooms unannounced as Tilly did. After allowing a few moments to pass, Emily finally entered.

The scene in the room was exactly the same as the last time she had been there. It was as if she had simply returned to look at a painting on the wall. Mrs. Poovey still sat silently by her cot in the same frayed black wool shawl, with her tiny hands folded in her lap. Across from her, the enormous Mrs. Loops overflowed a tiny wooden chair, her apricot dress, large as a circus tent, drooping about her ankles. Her face was stained with recent tears, and as Emily entered, fresh supplies were already preparing to gush from her eyes. Yet, like Mrs. Poovey, she said nothing. Except for an occasional sniff and a dab at her eyes with a sodden handkerchief, she sat and stared at the blank wall in mournful silence.

Emily set her bucket on the floor and knelt down beside it. Then, reaching in as if to pull out a rag or a sponge, she carefully lifted out the sleeping kitten instead. Without a word, she laid it gently on Mrs. Poovey's lap within the circle of the small, withered hands. A hush fell on the room as Mrs. Poovey continued to sit silent and still. Then slowly, slowly she lifted one hand and began to stroke the kitten's head. And then slowly, just as slowly, two tears welled in her eyes and rolled down her wrinkled cheeks.

"Does it have a name?" she asked. Her voice was like the tinkling of a tiny, very old silver bell.

"Not yet," replied Emily. "Would you like to give it one, Mrs. Poovey?"

Mrs. Poovey seemed to go into a trance as she continued stroking the kitten. "Clarabelle," she said at last, transporting the name from a faraway time and place. "I had a kitten by that name once."

"Then that shall be its name!" Emily said promptly.

With that, Mrs. Poovey suddenly took Emily's hand in hers and pressed it to her wet cheek. "Oh, my dear child! My dear child!"

Emily gave her a trembling smile. What would

Kipper say if he could see Mrs. Poovey, who had not been able to cry since she entered Sugar Hill Hall, now crying tears of happiness!

The continuously weeping Mrs. Loops, however, had most curiously not produced the smallest sniff for some moments. Emily turned to her, and there was Mrs. Loops beaming and holding out her arms for Clarabelle! Mrs. Poovey quickly handed her the kitten.

"Clarabelle is a lovely name, Mrs. Poovey. I couldn't have thought of a prettier one," said Mrs. Loops.

Mrs. Poovey's face, already wrinkled as a dried leaf, crinkled further with pleasure. "Thank you, Mrs. Loops."

These were probably the first words the ladies had exchanged since Mrs. Loops's arrival! After a few enchanted moments, in which the two simply sat gazing at the kitten asleep in the folds of Mrs. Loops's apricot dress, Mrs. Poovey spoke again.

"She has a pink nose!"

"And white whiskers!" added Mrs. Loops in the voice of one who has just made the most remarkable discovery in the world.

"Could—could she be purring?" asked Mrs. Poovey.

Mrs. Loops lowered an ear close to Clarabelle and nodded raptly.

They continued finding new delights about the kitten to bring to one another's attention and exclaim over, murmuring softly and hesitantly as if they were learning to talk all over again and needed to become used to the sound of their own voices.

Not wanting to interrupt the kitten's magic, Emily went quietly to work on her chores. The two old ladies were so intent on Clarabelle, they hardly seemed to notice that all the while they were talking, Emily was sloshing and washing, scrubbing and sweeping, bed making and dusting. She didn't mind at all and was perfectly content to let the kitten be the center of attention. After all, think what it had accomplished! She began to sing under her breath.

> *"Clarabelle's the kitten's name,*
> *Kitten's name, kitten's name,*
> *Nothing now will be the same,*
> *My fair lady!"*

Emily never even noticed that the room had fallen very quiet, and the ladies had stopped talking. Then suddenly Mrs. Poovey rose from her chair and took Emily's hands in her own.

"My dear child, thank you for bringing life to this barren room!"

"Oh!" breathed Emily. "You and Mrs. Loops *do* love the kitten so much, don't you?"

"Of course we do!" exclaimed Mrs. Poovey. "But darling Emily, it's *you* I meant!"

"Of course it was!" affirmed Mrs. Loops, returning Clarabelle to Mrs. Poovey in order to draw Emily down onto her own ample lap, hugging and petting her as if she were a kitten too!

"And just think of the danger in bringing Clarabelle to us!" The huge apricot lap under Emily trembled as if it were being shaken by a violent earthquake.

"Well, I wanted so much to have you smiling and talking. Mrs. Poovey, why did it take you so very long? I began to think you never would speak."

Mrs. Poovey traced a pattern on Clarabelle's head with a delicate finger. "I believe I had forgotten how, and I believe Mrs. Loops was rapidly forgetting, too, like all of us. And you must remember how very frightened we all are. So very, very frightened of this house and of everyone in it."

"Even of me?" asked Emily.

"Even of you, dear child—at first." Mrs. Poovey sent Emily a smile that begged her forgiveness.

"But Mrs. Poovey," Emily blurted out, "you dared to take the peppermints!" Then she gasped and threw her hands to her mouth. But it was too late, the words were out.

Mrs. Poovey stiffened. All sound was squeezed from the room by a silence as heavy as stone. The silence continued, until all at once it was shattered into a thousand tinkling bits by the sound of Mrs. Poovey's tiny, silver bell laughter. A mischievous spark twinkled in her eyes. "Why so I did!" she exclaimed.

"You didn't!" gasped Mrs. Loops, her extra chins quivering with delight.

"I did indeed!" retorted Mrs. Poovey.

"Well, I never!" said the beaming Mrs. Loops.

Emily would like to have stayed there the whole morning, enjoying this delightful scene, but she still had an entire attic-full of chores ahead of her. She slipped off Mrs. Loops's expansive lap. "Please excuse me, but I do have to go on with my work."

"Must you go so soon?" Mrs. Poovey asked. "It seems as if you've only just come."

"I've been here much too long already," Emily said. She picked up her bucket, and then thought of something. "Oh! Oh!"

"What's the matter, child?" Mrs. Loops asked anxiously.

"What am I going to do with Clarabelle while I do the other rooms?" Emily moaned. "I would love to take her with me for the others to see, but I can't. I haven't time. What shall I do with her?"

The two old ladies exchanged glances. "Why, leave her here with us, of course!" said Mrs. Poovey.

"Are—are you certain it's all right?" Emily asked.

"You needn't have a moment's worry, child," Mrs. Poovey said. "She'll be perfectly safe here, won't she, Mrs. Loops?"

"Oh, *perfectly!*" said Mrs. Loops.

৯৯

Emily's happiness over what had happened in Mrs. Poovey's and Mrs. Loops's room was thoroughly dampened when she had to slosh and wash and dust and sweep before the silent, hopeless faces of Mr. Bottle and Mr. Dobbs, Mrs. Quirk and Mrs. Biggs. If only the kitten could be brought around to all of them! But Kipper had said that Emily could keep it for no more than two nights, and that put an end to the matter. She finished her chores and hurried back to retrieve Clarabelle.

Persuaded that the kitten's safety was assured, Emily was stunned by the scene that met her when she returned to the room of the two old ladies. Both Mrs. Poovey and Mrs. Loops were sitting by their cots with faces as bleak and expressionless as two old stones. And Clarabelle was nowhere to be seen! But as Emily's eyes scoured the room with horror, Mrs. Poovey and Mrs. Loops suddenly broke into tremulous smiles.

"My dear child, we are so sorry if we frightened you," said Mrs. Poovey.

"Oh yes, dear, we only wanted to show you how very careful we would be if you—if you . . ." Mrs. Loops faltered, and turned to Mrs. Poovey.

"If you would only let us keep Clarabelle with us!" concluded Mrs. Poovey.

"K-k-keep Clarabelle?" stammered Emily. "Do you

mean not take her back at all?"

"That is exactly what we mean!" said Mrs. Poovey. "We promise to take such good care of her, and we do so much want to share her with the others."

Share Clarabelle with the others! Wasn't that what Emily had wanted? "But—but where would you keep her? Wouldn't it be too dangerous?"

Conspiracy twinkled in the look that danced from Mrs. Poovey to Mrs. Loops and back again. "Attics have all sorts of hidden nooks and crannies—" said Mrs. Poovey.

"Yes!" chimed in Mrs. Loops. "Behind doors and cupbo—" She stopped suddenly in blushing confusion as Mrs. Poovey sent her a warning cough.

"We think it safer, dear child, for you to know nothing about Clarabelle's hiding places." Mrs. Poovey paused before asking suddenly, "Does Tilly know of the kitten?"

"Oh no!" cried Emily. "No one knows of it except Kipper, who gave it to me."

"Good!" said Mrs. Poovey firmly. "Now, will you let us keep Clarabelle?"

Emily needed only a few moments to decide on her answer. "Yes!" How she would face up to an angry Kipper she would think about later.

The two ladies clapped their hands in little-girl delight.

"Now I must hurry back to the kitchen," Emily

said. "I'll try to come back later with food for Clara-belle."

"Splendid!" exclaimed Mrs. Poovey. "But please, dear darling child," she begged, "wait for one more moment. I want to give you a gift for all you have done for us." As she was speaking, she daintily lifted her skirt and unpinned something from her petticoat. "Here, it is all I have left of value in this world, but I do want you to have it."

Tears sprang to Emily's eyes as Mrs. Poovey pressed into her hand a small cameo brooch of coral set in pure gold.

"Oh, Mrs. Poovey, why didn't I think of doing that?" said Mrs. Loops. "How clever of you to have pinned the brooch to your petticoat. I would love to have something for Emily, but all my j-j-jewels were t-t-taken from my travelling bag before it came to this room." She pressed a handkerchief to her eyes.

Jewels taken from Mrs. Loops's travelling bag! Aunt Twice stitching Emily's twenty gold pieces into the mattress in her cellar room! A cameo pinned to a petticoat! Did every precious thing in Sugar Hill Hall have to be hidden lest it disappear mysteriously? What of Mama's jewels that were still to come in the trunks? Where were they to be hidden—or for that matter, this very cameo?

"Please, Mrs. Poovey, would you be so kind as to keep it for me? And my locket as well?" Emily unfastened it from around her neck. "I wouldn't want them—want them *lost*." She couldn't help thinking of Tilly reviewing all her "pretty things" in the cellar, and "borrowing" (probably forever) her white fur tam-o'-shanter. It was a wonder that she had thus far been able to keep her locket from Tilly's prying eyes.

"Lost? Lost indeed!" Mrs. Poovey bobbed her head indignantly. "Just as Mrs. Loops's jewels were *lost*, I expect. But of course I will keep both the cameo and the locket pinned safely to my person, dear child, and keep them safely. They might find a peppermint, but they won't tamper with a petticoat!" she added tartly. "And now you must hurry along."

"I will," Emily said. "But please, please do be careful!"

"You may be sure that we will, child. The walls of Sugar Hill Hall may have eyes and ears." Mrs. Poovey's own eyes, sharp as a bird's in search of a worm, darted around the room. "But then, so do we!" she concluded grimly.

ELEVEN

The Remembrance Room

Emily was on her knees scrubbing the kitchen floor when a strong smell of fish announced Kipper's arrival. He was cradling in his arms the familiar newspaper-wrapped parcel, but his normally cheerful face looked stricken.

"It's been found out, ain't it!" he exclaimed.

Emily barely looked up at him. "N-n-no," she stammered in a small, fading voice.

Kipper's clear eyes narrowed suddenly as he thumped the package of fish down in the sink. "All right, Emily, me girl, you'd best come clean with me. If it ain't been found out, and it ain't in the room where it was to stay—and it *ain't* because I *looked*—then where is it? Pa'll have my skin in strips if anything happens to you on 'count o' that kitten."

Emily finally gathered the courage to look Kipper in the eye. "It's—it's up in Mrs. Poovey's and Mrs. Loops's room."

"In Mrs. *Whats's* and Mrs. *Who's* room?" Kipper

exploded. "I *thought* you was acting mighty fishy, if you'll pardon the expression. What in thunderation is it doing up there after I warned you, Emily?"

"I had a *very* good reason." Emily sniffed indignantly.

"Well, it had better be!" Kipper produced as cold a look as someone with his cheerful red hair and cheeks could muster. "Perhaps you'd just best tell me 'bout it, *if* you don't mind."

"All right then," said Emily, "if you want to know, I wasn't going to take the kitten to show the old people, except that the very next meal after you gave it to me, I ate *all* my soup and every crumb of my lump of bread. So there!"

"Fish syrup!" said Kipper grimly. " 'Twas the fish syrup done that, *not* the kitten."

"It might have been *partly* the fish syrup, but it was *mostly* the kitten." Emily threw her chin up defiantly. "I carried it upstairs hidden in my cleaning bucket, and *I* never met *anybody*, and *it* never *mewed!*"

"Well," said Kipper, *"you* might have, and *it* might have, and what you done was stoopid, Emily!"

This lecture was followed by several minutes during which both parties sank into stony silence.

Then at last Kipper said gruffly, "All right, as long as you done it, you might as well tell me all 'bout it."

This was all the persuasion Emily needed. She was bursting to tell Clarabelle's story, and before she had finished, Kipper could no longer hide his grudging admiration.

"So have all the old ones seen the kitten now?" he asked.

"Not quite all," replied Emily, "but Mrs. Poovey and Mrs. Loops intend to see that they do, every one of them. And Kipper, you can't imagine how it is now when I go into the rooms where Clarabelle has been, everyone smiling at me and making conversation."

"And calling you a dear child, too, no doubt!" Kipper grinned. "I *suppose* you deserve it, so no need to blush 'bout it."

"Anyway," Emily continued when she had recovered from the blush, "Clarabelle will need some more fish and some milk and some sand, and—"

"And I ain't got a choice, I suppose, but to be the one to pervide all them necessities o' life?" inquired Kipper.

"Oh yes, please," said Emily quite matter-of-factly, as if the whole thing was settled and there was nothing more to be said about it.

Kipper could only stand and stare at her. It could be said that the kitten had, in fact, got his tongue!

"And there's something I haven't told you yet, Kipper," Emily said. "This morning at breakfast, all the old people finished their gruel, six asked for more, and some even began on their bread lumps. There now, tell me Clarabelle hadn't anything to do with it!"

"Dingus, Emily," said Kipper, "if you ain't the one!"

๑๑

The morning meal, the noon meal, and the evening meal were becoming livelier and livelier events, what with gruel, fish head stew, and soup being drained down to the bottom of the bowl, bread being eaten up so rapidly that in no time at all fresh bread had to be provided, and the secret smiles and glances that were passed along with the tea bag as it travelled around the table. Once, when Mr. Popple dropped the bag into his tin cup with a splash, a few small sounds of choked mirth were actually heard! Unfortunately, however, as mealtimes grew to be sunnier and sunnier occasions, the atmosphere around the head of the table grew darker and darker and frostier and frostier, like a storm cloud building up over the North Pole.

This worried Emily, but she could not see how Mrs. Meeching could possibly lock someone in the Remembrance Room for finishing a bowl of soup or a lump of bread, or for simply smiling. And Clarabelle remained safely hidden. Emily had no idea how it was managed. It seemed a miracle to her that when she arrived for her chores each day, there was never a trace of Clarabelle's existence anywhere. The kitten only appeared magically when it was determined that the approaching footsteps were Emily's alone.

One day Emily was bursting with still more news for Kipper. Mr. Dobbs had said he wished he had a whittling knife and a small bit of wood so that he could carve a likeness of Clarabelle. Mrs. Quirk wished for colored wool and a square of canvas to cross stitch the picture of a kitten that would in time be made into a pillow for Clarabelle. And as for Mrs. Poovey and Mrs. Loops, well, "Mrs. Poovey wants some watercolors to paint Clarabelle's portrait, and Mrs. Loops would like paper, pen, and ink to write a story about her! Almost all the old people want to make something that has to do with Clarabelle. Isn't that splendid, Kipper?"

"Splendid it may be, Emily," Kipper said, "but who got the money to buy all them things? I ain't got 'nough, even with my delivery jobs. I don't much like asking Pa for it, him not exactly being a millionaire nor anything like that. And you certainly ain't got any bankroll, Emily, as I can notice. So where would it come from?"

"I *do* have something!" Emily blurted out. She dropped her voice to a whisper. "I—I have twenty gold coins!"

Kipper's eyelids flew up so suddenly they almost lifted him off the floor. "Twenty gold coins? Come 'long, Emily, you ain't got any such thing."

"Yes, I do, Kipper! Aunt Twice and I hid them in—" Emily felt a firm hand clapped over her mouth.

"If you really do got any such pirate's treasure," Kipper said, scowling, "I don't want any knowledge o' where it's hid. Suppose, just suppose someone was to take it. Who would you think done it? Why the one who knowed where it was, that's who! But if you want to spend any o' that loot on the old people's paints and wool and all them things, why you just give me *one* o' them coins. It'll last a month o' Sundays. Then you just keep the rest close hidden, and don't tell *anybody* 'bout it."

So without even telling Aunt Twice, Emily carefully removed one gold coin from its hiding place in her mattress and gave it to Kipper. Soon carving, stitching and painting, modeling, weaving and crocheting were all busily embarked upon in the upper reaches of Sugar Hill Hall. Curiously, Emily never saw a trace of any of this activity going on, any more than she saw traces of Clarabelle. And yet when she arrived upstairs, Mr. Dobbs might show her a small piece of wood that was magically turning into a kitten, or Mrs. Quirk a whole square inch of cross stitches that somehow resembled a kitten's ear, or Mrs. Poovey a beautiful painting that came closer and closer to being Clarabelle every day.

The excitement over Clarabelle, suppressed though much of it had to be, for a while managed to take Emily's mind off the mysteries that shrouded the mansion. But they were like ghosts waiting in the wings, as in a play, for the right moment to reappear on the stage. And whenever Emily saw her pale, harried Aunt Twice, or received a trembling, secret smile from Mrs. Plumly, the ghosts were back to haunt her. She wanted desperately to tell them both about Clarabelle, but the two already shared a terrible secret. It would be cruel to bring another dangerous secret into their lives.

Emily saw no reason, however, why she should not visit Mrs. Plumly again, as invited, and she intended to do so. But she could never be certain when it was safe to knock on the closed door so the visit had not yet been paid. Then one day as she was climbing the stairs with her bucket, the door to Mrs. Plumly's room swung open, and Mrs. Plumly peered out cautiously, beckoning Emily to enter her room.

"I think we can feel safe for a few moments," she whispered. "Mrs. Meeching has gone out on an errand. I have some sad news, dear child, and I felt you should know of it. Mrs. Meeching has informed me that your trunks have been lost. Lost, hmmmph!" she said, sounding remarkably like Mrs. Poovey. "Stolen, more likely!"

"Stolen!" breathed Emily.

"Yes, indeed! And you in that poor, raggedly little dress. Mrs. Meeching will no doubt inform you that they were—*lost,* but I want you to know, child, that I will do all in my power to see that a warm dress is purchased for you."

A new dress could be purchased, but not Mama's

jewels! Should she tell Mrs. Plumly about them? Emily wondered miserably. No, she decided, better not. Mrs. Plumly was unhappy enough, and no need to add to her woe. The jewels were gone, and that was that. "Thank you, Aunty Plum!" was all Emily said, and she said it fervently.

Mrs. Plumly smiled. "I must say that in spite of that sad dress, you are looking so much better now, almost as if you were able to eat all the food placed on the table before you."

"Oh, I *am!*" cried Emily. It was all she could do not to tell, right then and there, about the fish syrup, Clarabelle, and all the activities now taking place just above their heads. But she said nothing.

"You aren't eating so much, dear child, that you would turn down a little cake and perhaps even a cup of tea—with lots of sugar and milk, of course!" Mrs. Plumly laughed. "Oh, the look on your face, child!"

Knowing that Mrs. Meeching was away seemed to make this visit so much pleasanter than the last. Emily had two lemon tarts and a chocolate cream eclair, and she and Mrs. Plumly talked and talked. They talked only about Emily's past, however, about her friend Theodora, her dear housekeeper Mrs. Leslie, and of course about Mama and Papa. They even laughed and giggled like schoolgirls together when Emily told of some of her pranks as a small girl, like the time she had hidden Mama's silver thimble. It had seemed so naughty then! Before Emily knew it, she had finished two cups of tea, was allowing a third to be poured, and had lost all track of time.

She might have stayed there the day if the doleful grandfather clock had not warned from the dining room that it was already eleven, and she had not even begun her chores. With a start, she jumped up from her chair. And it was at that exact moment that the door flew open, and Mrs. Meeching stood there!

"So this is what happens when I'm away, Mrs. Plumly!" Her face was contorted with pale rage.

Mrs. Plumly began to tremble violently. "I—I—"

"Silence! There is nothing you can say. *Nothing!* After all my kindness, all my generosity—entertaining this orphan brat no sooner I am out of sight." Mrs. Meeching turned to Emily and fixed her with a look of icy hatred. "Get out of my sight. Go to your room and stay there until you are sent for. Then you will see how those are dealt with who take advantage of their place in Sugar Hill Hall!"

With a shaking hand, Emily picked up her bucket and fled the room. When she heard the door slam behind her, it seemed to slam right on her breast, knocking out every last breath of air. That she herself might be punished, she had no doubt, but what, *what* would happen to Mrs. Plumly?

It was five terrible hours before an ashen-faced Aunt Twice appeared at the door to Emily's cellar room to inform her that they were all wanted in the parlor by Mrs. Meeching. Her heart thumping with terror, Emily scurried up the stairs behind her deadly silent aunt. But whatever Emily expected to find when she reached her destination, nothing in her wildest imagination could have matched the scene that greeted her when she finally stepped into the parlor.

Directly in front of the peppermints now stood a long, thin table pointing into the room like a sharp, accusing finger. Huddled to one side of it stood Mrs. Poovey and Mrs. Loops, Mr. Bottle and Mr. Dobbs, Mrs. Middle and Mrs. Odd, Mr. Popple and Mr. Quish, Mrs. Apple and Mrs. Quirk, Mrs. Dolly and Mrs. Biggs, Mr. Flower and Mr. Figg, and in fact every one of the old people, all staring at the table as if their frightened eyes were nailed to it. At the head of the table, her back to the peppermints, stood Mrs. Meeching, flanked on one side by Tilly, and on the other by Mrs. Plumly, who was not knitting, but looked instead as if she had turned to stone.

On the table before Mrs. Meeching, displayed as if in evidence for a criminal trial, was a large brown bottle of fish syrup Emily had left for safekeeping in Mrs. Poovey's and Mrs. Loops's room. Beside it, looking lost and lonely on that long table, lay Mrs. Poovey's cameo and Emily's locket.

But there was a great deal more. There were Mrs. Poovey's paints and her portrait of Clarabelle, Mrs.

Loops's pen and ink and writing paper, Mr. Dobbs's whittling knife and his small wood figure of a kitten, Mrs. Quirk's wool and cross-stitched picture, plus more paints, wool, thread, wood, and all the other pitiful bits and pieces resembling Clarabelle that the old people had been working on so diligently. And there, dangling by the scruff of her tiny neck from Tilly's rough hand, was Clarabelle herself!

So everything had been discovered. The eyes and ears of Sugar Hill Hall had done their work, and the one to be blamed for it all was Mrs. Plumly. Was it possible that her other terrible secret, the one guarded so carefully by both Mrs. Plumly and Aunt Twice, had been discovered as well?

For a few moments after Aunt Twice and Emily arrived, a deathly silence hung over the parlor. Then Mrs. Meeching's bloodless, pinched nose flared slightly, releasing one hiss of air for the benefit of all assembled, and her thin lips began to move.

"So you all thought you could get away with something, eh? Well, as you can see, you weren't nearly so clever as you thought. My walls have eyes, you know." As if to make certain no one missed this point, Mrs. Meeching's own eyes narrowed to cruel slits. "I thought you had all learned that *here* you do as *I* say, and no use complaining about it to anyone else. You are all only shadows, you know. Nobody sees you or thinks about you, especially the people who have brought you here.

They see you even less than anyone else, because they don't want to see you. And not wanting to see is the most effective kind of blindness, don't you know?"

Mrs. Meeching paused to fix each old resident of Sugar Hill Hall with a piercing stare. "So in the end, if you wish to complain, you had better complain to me." This said with all the sincere feeling of a rattlesnake. "As to the matter of punishment, you should all be thrown into the Remembrance Room for these crimes. Because there is one among you, however, whose crimes are so much greater than all the rest, you will be pleased to know that *she* will pay for all of you." At this, Mrs. Meeching suddenly drew herself up into a tight tower of rage. Her thin lips gripped her bony teeth, and her eyes became pinpoints of hatred.

"It is the person," she spit out, "who sneaked this cat into the attics of Sugar Hill Hall and who stealthily crept through the hallways poisoning its inhabitants with a loathesome concoction. It is the person who has grown fat on my bounty, and then repaid the kindness of my warm, generous heart with deceit and ingratitude. And that person, as you may well have guessed, is the conniving, vicious, vile *Emily Luccock!*"

A moment after the words rang out in the silent, cold, shadowy parlor, there was a loud thump as Mrs. Plumly, her eyes rolled up, fell to the floor in a dead faint. Aunt Twice gasped and clutched her throat. Until the moment Emily's name was spoken, both ladies must have thought *they* were the ones to be found guilty of the crimes. But it was Emily, and now the sentence was to be pronounced.

"For this treachery, the orphan brat's punishment will be: first, that she forfeit the nineteen remaining gold coins that she secretly and treacherously hid in her mattress." (Those discovered too! thought Emily.) "Second, that her partner in crime, that filthy fishmonger's boy, shall nevermore set foot in this place. And third, that she shall be locked in the Remembrance Room for twenty-one days, remembering how very good I have been to her, and what an ungrateful, evil child she is. As for the cat," hissed Mrs. Meeching, "take it out, Tilly, and drown it!"

Clarabelle to be drowned! Everything ended! And herself to be thrown into the Remembrance Room for twenty-one days! Numb with horror, Emily trailed after the tall, icy figure of Mrs. Meeching through the dining room, past the kitchen, down the stairs, up the dark passageway to the dreaded room at the end. A key grated in a rusty lock. A boneless hand caressed the door to the sound of a long, lingering hiss. The heavy door opened with a groan. A small, trembling body entered the room. The door clanged shut. The key turned again in the lock with a squeal of anguish, and Emily was enclosed in the deepest, darkest, coldest underground tomb of Sugar Hill Hall.

Who could have told the secret of Clarabelle,

Kipper's Pa's fish syrup, and even the nineteen gold coins? Emily's brain was too frozen even to think. But there was one thing she did know. When she had passed Tilly at the stairwell dangling poor, doomed little Clarabelle by the scruff of the neck, Emily had caught the distinct, definite, unmistakable breath of *PEPPER-MINT!*

TWELVE

A Midnight Visit

Somewhere, sounding so far off as to come from another world, a clock tolled the hour of twelve. Whether mid-day or midnight it might have been impossible to tell. The Remembrance Room had no outside windows and allowed only the barest whisper of flickering gaslight through the small square window in the door. Emily knew it to be midnight only because it had been afternoon when she was locked up.

Every bone in her body had begun to ache as she tossed restlessly on the hard wooden bench that served as a bed. She couldn't stop shivering under the miserably thin coverlet "pervided by the management," as Kipper would have said. And oh, how she would love to have heard his own voice saying it at that moment! All she had for company were her own grim thoughts drumming endlessly through her tired head, making sleep impossible. Clarabelle drowned. Everything ended. Twenty-one whole days and nights in the Remembrance Room. Clarabelle drowned. Clarabelle drowned. Drowned! Drowned!

How many times this parade of horrors had circled Emily's brain she had no idea, but the clock had not much more than stopped tolling when through the suffocating darkness she heard someone singing softly. The voice was so close it might almost have been in the same room.

> *"I've come to see you, Emilee,*
> *Emilee, Emilee,*
> *It's me come back from the* Fiddle Dee Dee,
> *My fair lady!"*

Emily scrambled from the bench and stumbled to the door.

"Kipper!"

A brass lantern appeared at the window, lighting up Kipper's smiling face. "None other!"

"But you're not supposed to be here!" Emily cried. "You're supposed to be banished from Sugar Hill Hall."

"So I been told," said Kipper cheerfully. "Your aunt told me, and then Tilly told me. And then case my ears weren't polished up good 'nough to hear all them warnings, the snake lady herself told me. First, o' course, she had to tell me all 'bout where you was, and why, and for how long. Then she said sweetly, 'Don't ever—*hisssss*—set a foot in Sugar Hill Hall again, vile fishmonger's boy!' Thems her exact words."

"So—so why *are* you here?" asked Emily.

"Well, so happens I ain't setting *a* foot in Sugar Hill Hall. I'm setting *two* feet, and I ain't had any warnings 'bout *that!* Further, though the snake lady's sly as a fox and mean as a viper, sometimes she ain't any smarter'n a woolly caterpillar. She forgot all 'bout asking me for this!" Grinning, Kipper held up a brass key for Emily to see.

Despite all that had happened to her, Emily could not help giggling. She giggled and giggled helplessly, but gradually the giggles became gasps for air, and at length became sobs. "Oh Kipper, I've been so stupid! I should have listened to you about the fish syrup and Clarabelle. Now the old people are worse off than ever, and Clarabelle has been—has been *drowned!*" Tears poured down Emily's cheek.

"I ain't able to do anything 'bout Clarabelle," Kipper said, "and I'm sad and sorry for losing that kitten. But I ain't blaming you for it, nor is Pa, for trying to help the old ones. And it ain't true that they're worse off. They all had a touch o' sunshine in their poor old lives, and who's to say they ain't a lot better for it. Here now, take this and dry your eyes, and no more crying 'bout the tuna what took off with the tide, as Pa always says."

Kipper handed Emily a ragged bit of cloth through the window to serve as a handkerchief. It smelled terribly of fish, but to Emily nothing could have smelled better in the whole world at that moment. She sopped up her eyes and nose and smiled tremulously at Kipper.

"That's more like it!" said Kipper. "Now, what we got to figger is how everything got told to the snake lady, meaning who done the deed. Not as how we can do much 'bout it now, but best we know who not to tell what to, and who to be extra careful 'round. Could it o' been one o' the old ones?"

"Never!" cried Emily.

Kipper shrugged. "One o' them *could* o' spilled a bean accidental like. Then all the rest come tumbling out."

Emily thought this over. "I—I don't think so." Then she said triumphantly, "Not one of the old people knew about my gold coins, or where they were hidden, so it couldn't have been any of them!"

"Whew!" Kipper wiped his brow. "For the same reason, couldn't o' been me either. Good thing I never 'lowed you to tell me 'bout that hiding place. You *see* how it would o' been?"

"Kipper!" said Emily indignantly. "I *never* suspected you, not for a moment. And I never even remembered not telling you about that hiding place—so there!"

"Well, good thing all the same!" Kipper grinned. "Come to think on it, your aunt knew."

"But she didn't know anything else," said Emily. "Besides, you *know* it couldn't have been Aunt Twice."

"Guess I do," Kipper said. "Well then, how 'bout Mrs. Plumly?"

"*She* doesn't know anything at all," replied Emily.

Kipper scratched his head. "All that's left then is them mysterious old Sugar Hill Hall eyes and ears everyone's always going on and on 'bout."

"Not—not quite all," said Emily. "There's—there's still Tilly."

"Oh, I never even considered old Til," said Kipper. "I mean, she ain't all that perfeck, but she ain't black-hearted 'nough to do a thing like this. Besides, she didn't have any knowledge 'bout anything any more'n Mrs. Plumly."

"She could have," insisted Emily. "She was snooping about the door the night Aunt Twice and I hid the gold coins. And she just *could* have caught the old people. You said once there was no one better than Tilly for ferreting out news."

"True," admitted Kipper. "But . . ." He shook his head doubtfully.

"And there's one more thing," said Emily. "Don't you remember those words you sang to me about Tilly telling for peppermints?"

"Yes, but—"

"Well," Emily interrupted firmly, "when I passed Tilly on the way to being brought down here, I smelled *peppermint*. And it came from *her*, Kipper!"

"Dingus!" exclaimed Kipper solemnly. "So 'twas Tilly after all. I never would o' believed it!"

As dismayed by this discovery as Emily was angered by it, Kipper left soon afterwards, although only because it was too dangerous to stay any longer. And he left with the firm promise of returning the next night with a bottle of fish syrup, which, as Pa always said, strengthened the spirit as well as the appetite. Then darkness closed in on Emily once more.

She had no sooner dropped into a fitful sleep, however, than she heard her name being called out. Somehow it seemed to be woven into a terrible dream she was having.

"Emily! Emily!" the voice said urgently.

She woke up all the way at last, but it took her moments to recover from the dread of remembering where she was. The sound of her name being called, however, did not disappear with her dream. It continued to tremble in the darkness, whispered over and over.

"Emily! Emily!"

Cautiously she looked toward the window in the door, and there in the flickering light of a candle, she saw Tilly's pale face and flat blue eyes staring at her.

"Go away, Tilly!" said Emily. "You're a wicked girl!"

"I ain't no such thing!" declared Tilly, her candle wavering dangerously. "And I couldn't sleep two winks for thinking on how you might believes I told, when I ain't the one at all!" Tilly sniffled miserably.

"Yes, you are!" cried Emily. "And there's no use lying about it, because when I passed you in the parlor, *I smelled peppermint*, Tilly, and I know where it came from!"

At that, Tilly's candle trembled even more violently. "Don't say nothing 'bout that to Mrs. Meeching. Promises as how you won't say nothing, Emily!"

"Why should I promise?" said Emily, who wouldn't have told Mrs. Meeching anything for her life.

"Because I never earned them peppermints by telling!" Tilly blurted out. "I *stoled* 'em, Emily! You mights o' noted how scairt I looked in the parlor. Well, that was 'cause I thoughts as how the whole shebanging meeting was 'bout *me!*"

Emily studied this a moment. "Well—"

"Please don't tell!" Tilly pleaded. "Anyways, I can proves I ain't so wicked as you thinks."

"How?" asked Emily.

Without a word, Tilly thrust something at Emily

through the tiny window in the door. The something was—

"*Clarabelle!*" Emily cried

Clarabelle! Clarabelle! Clarabelle!

"Oh, Tilly," breathed Emily, "you didn't drown her after all!"

"O' course not!" said Tilly indignantly. "I loves kittens. Cats, too. I wouldn't never drown no kitten, though it's worth my life hiding this one. And case you has any doubt further 'bout my feelings, I mights as well tell you I knowed 'bout her all 'long!"

"You didn't!" exclaimed Emily, burying her face rapturously in the kitten's soft fur.

"Did, too!" said Tilly. "I didn't know 'bout them gold coins, but I knowed 'bout the fish syrup from seeing it in your bucket one day, and 'bout what all the old people was doing, too. And I never told. I never did, Emily!"

"I believe you now, Tilly!" Emily cried. "I really do!"

"So can us orphings go on being friends?" asked Tilly.

"Yes, we can!" declared Emily with all her heart. "We really can!" She could hardly wait to tell this good news to Kipper .

She was so taken up with Clarabelle, however, and the startling new revelation about Tilly, it wasn't until the two of them had left, leaving her once again in the crushing darkness, that the grim question leaped back into her mind. If not Tilly, then *who?*

THIRTEEN

The Trapdoor

Bong! Bong! Bong! Bong! Bong! Bong! Straining her ears, Emily counted as the gloomy clock, muffled by endless layers of stone walls, knelled the hours into her dark cell. *Bong! Bong! Bong! Bong! Bong!* Eleven o'clock, and still no sign of Kipper. Of course, he had not arrived until midnight the night before, so there was time yet for him to put in an appearance. Emily shut her eyes tight, thinking that if she could doze off, the time would pass more quickly. Then all at once, her eyes flew back open. Voices! She heard the sound of voices breaking through the heavy silence from somewhere! Emily stiffened, staring wide-eyed into the darkness and listening.

Was somebody coming to see her? Neither Kipper nor Tilly nor Aunt Twice would be likely to let themselves be heard visiting the prisoner at this hour. Who then? It was impossible to tell. Like the clock, the voices were muffled, and they had a curious hollow echo to them. But there was something else quite startling about the voices. They seemed to be coming from somewhere *under the floor* of the Remembrance Room! Closer and closer drew the voices until they were almost under the bench where Emily lay, and then gradually they began to fade away until at last they disappeared altogether.

Emily shivered. Was the darkness playing tricks on her? How could voices be coming from under a cellar floor? It wasn't possible! In the end, persuaded that she must have become crazed from being alone in the dark and had imagined the whole thing, she drifted into a restless sleep.

She had no idea what time it had become when she was startled into sudden awakeness by the sound of a key grating in the rusty lock of her cell and then being carefully removed. Ready to feign sleep in a moment, she watched the door open slowly. A brass lantern with the wick turned down low appeared around the door, and right behind it was Kipper!

"Evening, Emily!" he said, calm as a sunny day at the shore, and just as cheerful.

Emily could only stare at him, speechless with happiness and surprise at seeing him right before her in the cell. Fear and the memory of strange voices imagined in the dark suddenly vanished.

"Come now, ain't you going to say anything? Tuna

got your tongue, as Pa always says?" Kipper grinned.

Emily threw her hands to her mouth. "Kipper!"

"Once again, as promised! Come to help you run away, Emily."

"Run—run away?" stammered Emily.

"That's right, run away to Pa's and my place," said Kipper. "Leastways 'til we could find a safer spot."

Run away! Emily had never considered the possibility. But now the door to her prison was unlocked, and she *could* run away. She had a place to run to, which was an enormous consideration, and someone to look after her. Run away—the answer to everything! Or was it?

"I—I can't," said Emily.

"*Can't!*" Kipper exploded. "Why not, Emily? This place addled your brain already?"

"I don't think so. It's just that . . . just that—"

"Just that *what?*" Kipper interrupted impatiently. "You best come up with some good explanation, Emily."

"Well, what do you suppose would happen if I ran away?" said Emily defiantly. "Mrs. Meeching would believe that someone in Sugar Hill Hall had let me out, and who would be punished for it? It could be anyone she chose—poor Aunt Twice, or poor Mrs. Plumly, or even one of the old people. It could be Mrs. Poovey or Mr. Bottle or—or *anyone!* So I can't run away, much as I want to. I *can't,* Kipper!"

Kipper scratched an ear. "Guess I never thought

'bout any o' that, Emily. But you're right, I'm blessed if you ain't. Danged snake lady! Well," he said with a deep sigh, "ain't much left to say excepting I *will* come see you as often as I can."

Emily struggled to keep a solemn face. "Someone else will be coming to see me often too."

"I expect you mean Tilly, who'll be bringing you your lumps o' bread and some o' the other outstanding Sugar Hill Hall wictuals," said Kipper. "I guess you ain't going to be too happy 'bout seeing *her,* for more'n one reason."

"For your information, I *will* be happy to see Tilly. Now what do you make of that?" Emily could no longer keep the happy smile from her face.

"What I make of it is that you're just as addled as you can be," replied Kipper. "What's Tilly done now, repent o' her wicked deeds?"

"It's what Tilly *hasn't* done, Kipper!" cried Emily. "She hasn't drowned *Clarabelle!*"

Kipper stared at Emily as if he'd been struck by lightning but hadn't fallen over yet.

"It's true," said Emily. "She brought Clarabelle to show me last night after you'd gone. That's the someone else I meant—not just Tilly, but Tilly and Clarabelle!"

Kipper finally blinked. "Well, I'll be a beached barnacle, as Pa always says!"

It was a long while before everything that could be said had been said about this wonderful news. But not until the subject of who had done the terrible deed of telling, if not Tilly, had been thoroughly, although unsuccessfully explored, did Emily finally remember something.

"Kipper!" she gasped. "I forgot to ask you—how did you get the key to the lock?"

Kipper grinned wryly. "I was commencing to think as how you never *would* ask! Mind if I take a seat?"

"Please!" said Emily.

They both perched on the hard bench with Kipper's little lantern between them, and he told his story.

"Happens on my way out last night, I get this sudden notion, so I hightail it right into the kitchen and pick me up a lump o' bread from the basket. I pour a dab o' water over it and mux it up real good 'till it's like a hunk o' clay. Then off I go with it to the snake lady's room."

"You didn't!" exclaimed Emily. She was already turning all goose bumps.

"I did!" said Kipper. "First I look, and there ain't any light coming from under the door. Then I listen, and there ain't any sound excepting the one o' the snake lady snoozing. I happen to know that sound on 'count o' one time when I was cleaning out her chimney, she dropped off, and she don't snore when she snoozes, she snarls. Spits, too, right through her teeth. So, hearing the familar snoozing tune, I open the door, which luckily ain't locked, and slide in slippery as a fish."

Emily, all attention, shifted nervously on the bench.

Kipper lowered his voice to a hush, thoroughly relishing the telling of his tale to such a responsive audience. "Well, there's her big ring o' keys hanging right on her bedpost. Ain't no need to ask anyone which key's the one to the Remembrance Room, 'cause it's standing out clearer than a whale in a bucket o' sardines, as Pa would say. So I lift up that key and press it into my muxed-up bread lump. I got me a perfeck image o' that key, and this here one's made right from that bread lump! What do you think o' that, Emily?"

"What—what I think of it is that you might have been caught, and you shouldn't have done it," said Emily, and then added in a rush of words, "but I'm so glad that you did!

Kipper beamed. After that, they just sat on the bench, swinging their legs happily. Then Kipper picked up his lantern and shone it around the room. The little spot of light explored the walls and ceiling, and finally arrived at the floor. There it stopped. The spotlight had discovered a darkened slab of wood fitted so closely into the stone floor it might have been part of the floor itself, except that it was fastened on one side with a heavy, rusted padlock. Emily started when she saw it.

"Hey!" Kipper exclaimed softly. "Look at that, Emily. 'Pears to me to be the cover o' some kind o' well. But what's a well doing here?"

"Long, long ago," Emily said, "I remember Uncle Twice telling Papa of a well in the cellar of Sugar Hill Hall. He said he had never even bothered to open it up since it wasn't needed. This might be that well, Kipper. But . . . but—"

"But what, Emily? Why do you got that pecoolyar look on your face?"

"I—I—I," Emily stammered. "Oh, Kipper, if I tell you, you'll say I'm addled again. I thought I was addled, too, and had imagined the whole thing."

"What whole thing?" asked Kipper impatiently. "Ain't any way I can decide 'bout it if you don't tell me, Emily."

"Well, some time before you came tonight, about eleven o'clock, I heard voices, and it seemed as if they came from under the floor. From under this very room, Kipper!"

"Voices?" Kipper looked curiously at Emily. "From under this room?"

"There!" exclaimed Emily. "You see, you do think I'm addled!"

"No such thing, Emily!"

"You—you mean you believe I *did* hear them?"

Kipper nodded. "O' course I do! I ain't surprised 'bout anything that could happen in this spooky mansion. Did you hear what the voices was saying."

"They were too far away and hollow sounding," Emily replied. "But—but do you suppose there might be another cellar under this one and not a well at all? Perhaps Uncle Twice just *thought* this was a well."

"Ain't anyone ever told me 'bout any cellar deeper'n this one, Emily, but that ain't to say that there ain't one. Nobody told me 'bout any well either."

Kipper studied the old slab of wood, and then suddenly was down on his knees beside it. He twisted the old lock in his hands, and after he had studied it for a moment, tried jabbing his key into it. The key fit! Quickly, he wiggled it back and forth. There was the squeal of metal against rusty metal, and the old lock finally released its ancient, rusty grip. Kipper looked up at Emily with wild, excited eyes. "Now we'll see what we shall see!"

"Be careful!" Emily cried. "If it *is* the well—"

"I ain't going to drop into any old well. Never fear!" said Kipper. He removed the lock and then, with several sharp tugs and a long pull, lifted the heavy slab of wood. Clouds of choking dust flew out at the edges. Holding up his lantern, Kipper peered down over the ledge into the black hole.

"Dingus, Emily!" he breathed. "This ain't any well. It's steps going down someplace! Come look."

Emily inched over toward Kipper. A moment later, she was looking down a flight of stone steps so long and blackened with filth and age they seemed like stairs to the middle of the world.

"Hello-o-o down there!" Kipper called out softly.

"Down there, down there, down there," came echoing back.

"That's a *long* stairwell," he said. "If it goes to any other cellar, must be one what's a jillion miles down." He waved his lantern, and eerie shadows danced on the ancient steps.

"Would—would you like to go see what's there?" asked Emily.

"Would *you?*" Kipper asked right back. His eyes were huge in the lantern light.

Emily hesitated a moment, and then finally nodded.

"All right then!" Kipper gulped. "I'll go first with the lantern."

As if some unknown horror was going to rise from the pit and grab him by the leg, Kipper put a hesitant foot on the first step and started down. Emily followed as close as she could behind him. It seemed half a mile later before they set foot off the last step and Kipper raised his lantern over his head to shine it around them.

"*Wheeoo!*" He gave a long, low whistle. "It ain't a well *nor* a cellar. It's a tunnel! Looks like the inside o' a serpent's belly, don't it?" Kipper spoke with all the authority of having seen several. "Look at them walls black with the breath o' his fire, and that slime oozing out o' his innards."

Emily shivered uncontrollably. The feeble glow of the lantern was barely able to break through the chill dark air, heavy with mold and decay, to pick out here and there the evil gleam of the slimy walls. It seemed as if she and Kipper must surely be the first living things to have entered the serpent since it turned to rock centuries earlier. But as Kipper slowly lowered the lantern to shine it on a rough kind of path under them, its light picked up a tiny sparkle from something lying at their feet. Emily stooped quickly to pick up the small object that made it, and then held out her hand to Kipper. In it lay a brass button marked with stars and anchor. It was dented from having been stepped on heavily, but hardly tarnished, as if it had only recently fallen there.

"Captain Scurlock?" Emily whispered, questioning.

"Maybe," Kipper said. He lifted the button from Emily's hand and held it close to the lantern. "Or one o' his ugly crew. But doing what? Looks like more questions, Emily." He shoved the button in his pocket and then raised the lantern, shining it to the left of where they stood. The light revealed a solid wall of blackened rock only a few feet away. "See? Ain't any way out o' this tunnel excepting the way we just came down, and we both know there ain't anyone but us has used them steps in a long, long time. Looks like they just been using this as a meeting place, though beats me *why*. There's lots cozier places in this world."

Kipper paused to shine his lantern in the opposite direction. The light hit a solid wall as well, but only of darkness, not rock. "This is where they come from, Emily, whoever they be. I got to admit, I'm scared to go on. But right now curious is getting the better of coward. You game to go on?"

Emily wanted to shake her head. She did not want to go into that terrifying blackness. But there were still questions, so many questions, to be answered. What if the tunnel would provide the answers? One answer. *Any* answers.

"I—I'm game," Emily said.

"Thought you would be," said Kipper.

They started down the grim, dark tunnel.

FOURTEEN

The Jolly Sailor

The darkness in the tunnel seemed dense as stone. Kipper's small lantern light bobbed about with hardly more effect than if he'd been holding a firefly on a chain. They could barely see the pools of murky water that lay along the path under still, deadly grey vapors, the evil breath of the sleeping serpent. Two rats scurried by, sending a cold rush of air up their legs. Emily stifled a shriek, and the lantern in Kipper's hand shook violently. But nobody suggested going back. They simply went on.

And on. With blackness closing in behind them, and blackness barely opening ahead, there was no way of telling how far they had come or how far they might have to go, twisting and turning. There was no way to measure time or distance. But just as Emily began to wonder if they might not wander down the tunnel forever, Kipper clutched her arm.

"Look, Emily!"

They had finally arrived at a flight of steps that was a twin to the one by which they had climbed down into the tunnel.

"Are we going up them?" Emily whispered.

"Looks like we ain't got anyplace to go but up, or back," Kipper replied. "See, Emily, beyond them steps is a rock wall same as the other. Appears the tunnel runs from where we come from to where we got to, and no more."

They stood still a moment, looking up and listening. There was only silence from above. Then Kipper motioned to Emily and began to climb the steep stairs. When he reached the trapdoor overhead, he drew a deep breath and pushed the door up a crack. Then he gave a low whistle. *"Wheeoo!"*

"What is it, Kipper?" Emily asked.

"Dingus, Emily!" Kipper turned to her with the oddest expression on his face. "I think what we just arrived at is the cellar o' the tavern near Pa's fish shop."

Emily didn't know whether she wanted to laugh or cry over this discovery. All that treacherous journey only to end up at a place near Kipper's home! And the comical look on Kipper's face!

Kipper peered through the trapdoor again. "Now I'm certain as I can be. We've come to the cellar o' The Jolly Sailor, which I run errands for and the like. This is where the wine and the spirits get kept. Why, dead ahead's that big old keg what's been warmed by my bottom more times than a fish flaps his fins, as Pa always says. Come 'long, Emily, let's go on up!"

They scrambled quickly through the open trapdoor, and then Emily was able to study the room they entered. Two whale oil lamps on the walls dimly lit up row upon row of waiting bottles, staring across the room at one another with vacant cork eyes. Huge blackened kegs studded the floor with no semblance of order at all, as if they were the abandoned toys of a giant's child grown tired with his game. It was like nothing Emily had ever seen before, until suddenly her eyes fell on something totally familiar, something she had climbed over time and again in her own family attic.

"Kipper!" she cried. "My two trunks over there in the corner! What are they doing *here?*"

She threaded her way around the giant kegs to where the trunks lay. Kipper ran to her side. The locks had been pried off both trunks, so it was an easy matter to lift the lids and look in.

"Empty!" said Kipper with disgust. "Beats me what the scurvy lot what frequents this 'stablishment wants with silk dresses and lace petticoats no bigger than would fit a tadpole. And ain't anybody what can get much payment for old clothes no matter how fancy they once was."

"But Kipper," Emily said, "it wasn't just my clothes in the trunks. All Mama's jewels were in the trunks, too! Everything!"

Kipper's jaw fell open. *"Wheeoo!"* he whistled. "Well, ain't no explaining *how* the trunks got here, but ain't any question *why*. I wonder 'bout—" He was interrupted by a sudden, wild explosion of laughter bursting down the cellar passageway.

"Another whoop-de-do going on in the private room," said Kipper darkly. "I ain't ever been 'lowed in there, but from the looks o' the crew what *is*, that Cap'n Scurlock being one, I ain't missing much. You know, Emily, once I—"

Kipper was interrupted again by another burst of ugly laughter, one that this time caused him and Emily to turn to one another with looks of dismay and horror. For somewhere in that laughter, they had heard the unmistakable, blood-chilling, all-too-familiar sound of a hisssss!

"I aim to go see what's up," Kipper whispered. "There ain't much light in the passageway, and plenty o' kegs to hide behind." Without even waiting for

Emily's opinion of this plan, Kipper darted for the door. A moment later, he had disappeared.

Emily had no intention of waiting there alone. She raced after him, following as he slipped like an eel from keg to keg toward a sharp shaft of light that stabbed through a partly open door. Crouching behind a large keg, they peered into the room.

Around a long, scarred oak table laden with a ham, a roast beef, a turkey, and all sorts of puddings, cakes, and custards (a collection, in fact, of the delectable foods Emily was used to seeing in the locked icebox), sat the grisly Captain Scurlock, his crew of rough officers, and two other persons. One of these, as they had guessed it would be, was Mrs. Meeching. With one hand under her sharp chin, and the fingers of another coiled around a long pipe, whose smoke glided silkily up her thin nose, she lounged in a carved black chair at the *foot* of the table.

But, unlike the first day she had entered Sugar Hill Hall, it was not Mrs. Meeching that caused Emily's blood to turn to ice in her veins. This time it was a second person, a person who sat in a chair raised from all the others as if on a platform at the *head* of the table. The face of the person was one Emily had loved. No, not the face of Uncle Twice, but the face of a woman. Vanished, however, was the sweet expression, the soft eyes, and the gentle mouth. The face was now a curiously twisted hard mask, the eyes glittering like blue glass marbles, and the mouth no more than a black hole lined with red, opened wide to pour out a howl of ugly laughter.

Emily turned to Kipper with horror. "Aunty Plum!"

"Locked up there in the Remembrance Room remembering her bad deeds, oh, it does my tender heart good!" shrieked Mrs. Plumly. "And when I think of her sitting there prim as you please drinking her Aunty Plum's nice, warm t-t-tea-hee-hee!" She exploded again with coarse laughter. "Never suspecting what was in it and pouring out all her tender little secrets about Mama's thimble and Papa's cap, getting tipsier and tipsier, and spilling out her nasty little tricks regarding the fish syrup, the old buzzards in the attic, that filthy cat, and her nineteen gold coins. 'Sewn up in my mattress, Aunty Plum,' she whispered to me, pleased as pleased could be."

So *Mrs. Plumly* was the evil behind the evil, the eyes and ears of Sugar Hill Hall, which had been told nothing, but seen and heard everything. And now it was known how!

As Mrs. Plumly spoke, her face grew uglier and uglier until she was spitting out the words. "Meal-mouthed, meddling little brat! I'd like to have my hands on those precious clothes of hers so I could have the pleasure of hurling them into this fireplace all over again. Well, she'll come out of the Remembrance Room a different child than she went in, mark my words. And if she gets any more dangerous ideas, there's always another cup of tea in Aunty Plum's room, eh, Meeching?"

"Indeed, Plumly!" said Mrs. Meeching in a fawning voice.

Then a poisonous smile spread over Mrs. Plumly's face. "I must say I've never done a finer acting job. But then I didn't earn my title of Queen of the Dance Halls for nothing, eh?"

"That was a splendid drop you did in the parlor, Plumly. Sssimply sssplendid!" hissed Mrs. Meeching.

"Ah yes!" mused Mrs. Plumly. She went into a trance, but quickly collected herself. "Well, perhaps on that note we had better take leave and be on our way."

The two ladies rose, the officers stumbled to their feet, and Emily felt a sharp tug on her arm. "Ain't got time to lose! Let's get back to the tunnel!"

Numb with horror and shock, Emily could barely make one leg follow the other as she slipped silently down the passageway with Kipper. It was not until they were back in the tunnel with the trapdoor safely down overhead, that her throat unlocked enough for her to speak. "Oh Kipper, how could I have been so stupid as to believe her!"

"Now see here, Emily," said Kipper sternly as they began their journey back up the tunnel, *"anyone* would o' believed her. She's a perfessional actress. And how was you to know you was guzzling tea which weren't just tea? There ain't any use banging your head 'gainst a wall to punish yourself for what ain't your fault. Anyways, we learned a couple o' somethings out o' this visit. 'Pears as how Mrs. Plumly is chief viper 'round Sugar Hill Hall, and not the snake lady. And also 'pears as how she ain't the one your Aunt Twice is pertecting."

"Which means that—that it might be Uncle Twice after all!" Emily's voice broke.

"Maybe," said Kipper. "*More*'n maybe, most likely."

"But how does Aunt Twice know he's really alive?" Emily cried. "Suppose he isn't and they've just been lying to her all along!"

"There you go with more supposings, Emily," said Kipper.

"Yes, but—but if he's alive, then where *is* he?" Emily was close to tears.

"That's what we got to find out," said Kipper. "But right now we'd best hurry you back to the Remembrance Room and me out o' it in case them two ladies decides to pay you a visit. You know, you could o' knocked me over when I seen them in The Jolly Sailor. I ain't ever seen them going in, nor out either. Beats me how they sneak in and out so secret. O' course—"

Kipper was interrupted by the distant, but loud,

clap of the trapdoor behind them being slammed shut. Footsteps tapped sharply on the stone stairs, and a moment later the screeching, hissing voices of Mrs. Meeching and Mrs. Plumly echoed hollowly down the tunnel.

"What the—!" exclaimed Kipper softly. "Them loony vipers is usin' the tunnel! Come on!" He grabbed Emily's hand and nearly pulled her off her feet. "We better move faster'n we ever done in our lives!"

If the trip down the tunnel had been terrifying, not knowing what was before them, then the trip up the tunnel was ten times more so, knowing what was *behind* them. Stumbling on the rocky path, gasping for breath in the stagnant air, they ran. But the twists and turns of the tunnel protected them, and the loud, echoing voices of Mrs. Meeching and Mrs. Plumly drowned out the sound of their footsteps. When they reached the stairway to the Remembrance Room, they scrambled up the stone steps and hurled themselves into the room. Then they swiftly, but carefully, *carefully* lowered the trapdoor and flattened themselves on top of it like two panting, trembling small animals who have just escaped their hunters, listening. The voices came nearer.

And nearer. They paused at the foot of the stairs to snarl and hiss for a few moments. Then the voices moved on in the direction of the stone wall. And disappeared!

Kipper stared round-eyed at Emily. "Them two ain't elves what can vanish. Must be steps what we missed."

"Steps?" said Emily. "To where?"

Kipper shrugged. "Beats me."

Then Emily gasped. "Do—do you suppose they lead into the ballroom? It should be just about overhead, Kipper."

"Dingus, Emily, you could be right!" exclaimed Kipper. "O' course, it's more rightly the ballroom what *was*, 'cause ain't likely any balls is being held there now, what with no windows and doors what we know of. More like a tomb, if you ask me."

Kipper had no sooner said the words than his face froze. "I—I'm sorry. I shouldn't o' said that, Emily."

"It's all right," Emily said quickly. "I—I've already thought it—that Uncle Twice might be in that room, buried alive."

Or dead! Wasn't that a possibility, too? But nobody said it. The words weren't necessary. The thought filled the small room like a crushing stone.

FIFTEEN

A Necklace of True Pearls

The distant clock tolled the hour of one o'clock in the morning as Emily tossed and turned restlessly on the hard bench. Where was Kipper? Why hadn't he come at midnight just as before? He had promised he would be there. What could have happened to him? The minutes dragged slowly by, and another half hour passed. Then suddenly there was the familiar sound of a key grating in the lock. Joyfully, Emily jumped from the bench and ran to the door.

It was Kipper, just as she had expected, but what a different boy he appeared *this* time. His head was a mat of dishevelled red curls, with some clinging damply to his forehead in small, wet corkscrews. His eyes were huge, and he was panting heavily as if he had been running hard and fast for a long distance.

"What is it? What's happened?" Emily cried. "Is someone after you?"

Kipper shook his head dazedly. "No, 'tain't anything like that, Emily. But there's more dark, mysterious goings-on afoot, and all got to do with you!"

"M-m-me?"

Kipper nodded. "And what you got to do now is come with me, 'cause you been sent for."

Emily started. "S-s-sent for?"

"Oh, no need to fear. 'Tain't by the snake lady or Mrs. P., but by an indiwidual what don't want to be made known to you 'til he's spoke his case."

Emily felt as if all the blood had suddenly been drained from her body. "U-U-Uncle Twice?" she breathed. "Kipper, did you find Uncle Twice?"

Kipper's eyes filled with sympathy. "No, 'tain't your Uncle Twice, Emily. But you got to come anyways, and no 'don't,' nor 'won't,' nor 'can't.' No use minding the old folks right now, much as you'd like, 'cause there's *others* with lives hanging on it, namely you and your Aunt Twice!"

"But what of *Uncle Twice's* life?" whispered Emily faintly.

"I don't know anything 'bout that, Emily. All I know's this indiwidual's waiting for you at Pa's place. Pa sent 'long one o' his own old seagoing jackets. He knows as how you'll get lost in it, but he says 'twill keep you warm. Besides, 'twouldn't do to go wearing velvet coats nor fur collars in the part o' town we got to cross to get to Pa's."

Emily took from Kipper a navy blue jacket faded by salt and sun and thick with the smells and stains of a thousand journeys over the sea. Kipper's Pa's jacket! The thought of being wrapped in this comforting object was the only thing holding Emily up at that moment.

"Don't put it on just yet," Kipper said quickly. "You can leave it here, 'cause first we got to make a visit to a place in Sugar Hill Hall to find some papers what this indiwidual says he got to have. And the papers is in that ballroom you been talking 'bout, Emily!"

The ballroom! They were going into it at last! "But how—how will we get there?" Emily asked.

"Same way as what the snake lady and Mrs. P. got there, through the tunnel, up the stairs, and through the trapdoor. We unlock it with this, what the indiwidual gave me!" Kipper held up a large tarnished brass key. "We can go in safety, 'cause the ladies ain't in residence, being at this moment in the cellar o' The Jolly Sailor. But we ain't got time to waste."

Even before he had finished speaking, Kipper was on his way down the stone steps into the tunnel. Emily hurried after him. It took them only moments to find the second steep stone stairway, which was hidden in a small cavelike room directly behind the stairs to the Remembrance Room. It was easy to see how this second flight of stairs could be missed.

Halfway up, however, Emily's footsteps faltered. "Oh, Kipper!" There was a sob in her throat.

"I know what you're thinking, Emily. You're thinking o' what might be on top o' that trapdoor what ain't papers," Kipper said. "Right now, howsumever, we ain't got any choice but to see."

He lifted the trapdoor carefully, peered under it, and then whistled. *"Wheeoo!* Come take a look o' this, Emily!"

Standing beside Kipper, Emily looked at last upon the ballroom that had once been the source of so much pleasure. But even though the walls were faded and the mirrors tarnished, the flickering light from several gas lamps now danced on a startling display of color and magnificent beauty that far outdistanced anything she had ever seen there before. Shimmering emerald green, scarlet, royal blue, and purple brocades lay spread around the room like sleeping silk serpents. Carved tables of teak, mahogany, and rosewood bore delicate cloisonne and porcelain vases, and bowls carved of precious turquoise, jade, and rose quartz. But what perhaps was the most dazzling of all were the shelves and tables sparkling with diamond and ruby necklaces, heavy chains of gold and silver, emerald and sapphire brooches and rings, and other exotic jewels whose names could only be guessed. It was a scene to take anyone's breath away. But beyond all this display worth two king's ransoms, the room was empty.

"No Uncle Twice!" Emily whispered. The ballroom had seemed to offer the last hope of ever finding him, and now all hope was gone. "He really *must* be dead. I know it now."

"You don't know any such thing," said Kipper staunchly. "Ain't anybody said he was in this room for certain. He'll come to light one o' these times, hale as a halibut and fit as a flounder, as Pa always says." These words of cheer were, unfortunately, not matched by the look on Kipper's face.

There was no time now, however, for sorrow or sympathy. Kipper's eyes quickly searched the room. "Oho! There 'tis, right over yonder by that—that *door!*" His voice exploded. "By dingus, Emily, there *is* a door, and it leads right into the snake lady's room, all nice and disguised by a wardrobe. Always wondered 'bout that second wardrobe with the big lock. Well, now I know!" He darted through the tables, making his way toward the large, heavily carved black desk in the corner.

Emily ran after him, but as she did, she suddenly saw something on a table that gave her heart a sharp stab of joy, mingled with a terrible sadness at the same time. "Kipper!" she cried. "Here is Mama's necklace of true pearls, given to her by Papa when I was born.

I'd know the clasp anywhere. Papa had it made especially with my initials, E. O. L., for Emily Ophelia Luccock."

"Stole from your trunk, o' course, Emily!" Kipper exclaimed over his shoulder. He was busy pulling out one drawer after another in the desk. "I trust you ain't surprised. That's what all this loot is 'bout—stealing and smuggling. I expect smuggling is how that brass button from a seaman's uniform come to be in the tunnel. A mighty cozy arrangement, I'd say, a tunnel running right up to this mansion. Oho again!" He lifted out a large sheaf of papers from the bottom drawer. "See, Emily, see here!" He pointed excitedly to the top sheet. "Says 'Luccock.' That's exactly what this individual wanted. Come on! I got 'em now, so let's go."

Hesitantly, Emily set the pearl necklace back on the table where she had found it.

"Ain't you going to take it with you?" Kipper looked astonished.

"Would—would it be all right?"

"If you ain't the one, Emily! O' course it's all right. They're yours, ain't they? They was property stolen from you. Here, I'll pin 'em on you."

As Emily felt the beloved pearls being clasped around her neck, tears flew to her eyes. These pearls had once been worn by Mama, and might be all she would ever have of her past. Even her present now had a question mark after it, because who knew what would come from this mysterious journey with Kipper. Question following question. Was there ever to be an end to them, or to the horrors of Sugar Hill Hall?

SIXTEEN

The Scary Indiwidual

This was Emily's first exit from Sugar Hill Hall since her arrival there, and all she was doing was going from a known terror to an unknown one. Even inside the comfort of Kipper's Pa's great coat, she shivered.

A night fog, thick as fish chowder, hung over the city of San Francisco. Emily could barely see Kipper right beside her as they crept from the back door of the mansion, out past the coach house, and down an alley to the street. Once out of the alley, Kipper's footsteps flew over cobbles long familiar to them. And so intent was he in reaching his destination, he suddenly grew silent as the fog.

Emily had to struggle to keep up with him, her breath snatched from her throat, and her feet aching from the hard stones. *Thump! Thump! Thump!* Was the sound of her footsteps real? Or had she finally become that ghost outside the train window, seeking but never finding a home? Gaslights flickering palely through the fog, and an occasional dark shadow borne past them on the muffled drum of horses' hoofs only made Emily feel more than ever that she had entered another world. *Thump! Thump! THUMP!* The cobblestone tripping Emily was all too real. With a gasp, she reached out for Kipper.

Kipper snatched her arm before she could fall. "Well, if I ain't the stoopidest! Going 'long with my noggin buried in the fog. I plain forgot you ain't ever been on these streets before."

Emily was happy to feel Kipper's warm reassuring hand close around her cold one. But it was still impossible to keep from feeling frightened as they plunged through the dark streets. And the journey became even more treacherous when they left the part of the city that had long since gone to sleep and arrived at the part that would not go to sleep until dawn.

The streets there teemed with life, but a kind of life Emily would not have recognized from her darkest dreams. She could almost wish she were back in the Remembrance Room as Kipper pulled her past dingy store windows, dark, evil doorways, and doors that swung open to let escape bursts of coarse laughter. She felt a terrible chill inside at the sight of the faces swirling around her—brutish bearded faces under strange-looking caps; pockmarked faces with slanted eyes; hideous flat faces without noses and with too-thick lips; and ladies' faces as brittle and bright as painted china plates.

Emily shuddered and then felt Kipper's hand tighten around hers. "Told you 'bout this part o' town, Emily. Ain't the best at any time, but night is when the rats come up from the sewers o' San Francisco. But we're 'bout there, so don't give up."

Kipper was right. Soon they reached the waterfront and a row of shops which, unlike the others they had just passed, had been put to bed for the night. Here it was quiet enough for water to be heard lapping softly against the wharfs.

"And here 'tis!" Kipper pointed proudly to a small darkened shop with a sign over it in the shape of a fish so large it looked as if it could swallow the shop and everyone in it in one bite. Kipper let go Emily's hand to unlock the door.

"Come 'long, Emily, this way!" Kipper beckoned to a staircase at the back of the little shop. Only one dim light burned inside, so Emily could gather the barest impressions of wooden kegs and vats neatly laid out in front of a tiny counter, but she could feel the friendly sawdust under her feet like a welcoming carpet. If only her first visit to Kipper's Pa's shop could have been under brighter circumstances!

"Pa! Pa!" Kipper called out softly as he climbed

the worn treads, with Emily close behind. "Pa, are you there?" Silence was his only reply.

Now they entered a small, cozy room that could have passed for a ship's cabin, except for one bright pink geranium blooming in a round window over the sink. The window looked so much like a porthole Emily was surprised not to see waves dashing against it. A ship's oil lamp on the wall and a fluttering candle on the table lit the room. But the only sign of life apparent was a small boy seated on a bench by the scrubbed pine table, his head laid down on it, and his tousled blond hair tumbling over his hands. He was fast asleep. Was this the scary, nameless "indiwidual" Emily had been brought to see? It was almost a cause for laughter.

"Little Shrimper! Little Shrimper, wake up!" Kipper shook his shoulders gently. "Where's Pa?"

Little Shrimper rubbed his eyes sleepily. "Gone for someone, Kipper. Don't know who, 'cause it were a name whispered to him by . . ." He jerked a thumb toward the bunk beds in a corner of the room.

Emily's eyes followed the direction of the small thumb, and she began to tremble. What she had thought was simply a mountain of bed quilts and blankets on the lower of the two bunks, now suddenly rearranged itself into what it truly was, the figure of a man!

"It's who you come to see, Emily," Kipper said soberly. Then he turned back to Little Shrimper. "He ain't dead yet, is he?"

Little Shrimper's eyes widened into big, round O's. Clearly, *death* was not something he had bargained for. "Pa didn't say so."

"Then he probably ain't." Kipper strode toward the bunks and lit a small oil lamp that hung on the bedpost. Then he leaned over the lower bunk to hold out a testing finger. "No, he ain't," he concluded matter of factly. He beckoned to Emily.

"This ain't going to be pleasant, but you best come see what you was brung for, Emily. This here's the indiwidual what wants to speak his case to you, though don't look like he's able right now."

Emily hesitated, but she knew that in the end she would have to make that short but terrible journey. Slowly, she crossed the room. When she arrived at the bunk, she took one quick look at the man lying stiff and still as a log, and her breath stopped in her throat.

She had seen his face only twice before, but on her mind had been carved forever the rubbery lips, the bulbous nose decorated with a large black wart, and the hideous gash running from cheek to chin. Now, under this face turned grey as an oyster shell, a stain on the chest of his seaman's uniform was opening up like a swift-blooming blood-red rose.

"Captain Scurlock!" Emily whispered. She had to turn her eyes from the sight.

"No other," said Kipper. "Sorry to o' had to do this to you, Emily, but he was 'fraid if you knew who 'twas wanted you, you might likely not o' wanted to come."

"But how did he get here?" Emily asked. "What is this all about?"

"Well—" Kipper rubbed an ear thoughtfully. "Since the Cap'n ain't in a present condition to speak his piece, and Pa ain't back yet, I guess I can tell you what I know. Let's set at the table with Little Shrimper. Pa's got water boiling, so I can fix us a nice cup o' tea with one whole lump o' sugar in it, *each!*"

"Me too?" piped up Little Shrimper.

Kipper smiled at him. "You too!"

Emily fell gratefully onto a bench by the table, happy to be able to leave the sight of the dread apparition on the bunk.

"Oh, come to think on it, Little Shrimper, this here's Emily what generously donated the peppermint to you," Kipper said cheerily. That he was shading the truth a bit didn't seem to concern him.

Little Shrimper stared at Emily with round eyes. Then he dipped into a well-worn pocket and pulled out a filthy rag, which he promptly laid open. Inside rested the peppermint, or at least what remained of it. "And I still got it, too!" he said proudly. "I only sucks a bit on it 'fore bedtime. Might even last 'nother week!" At that moment, Emily wished she had a hundred more peppermints to fill that little pocket!

"Now," said Kipper, setting down three mis-

matched pottery mugs of steaming tea, "the story begins
with me visiting the cellar o' The Jolly Sailor 'fore
coming to the Remembrance Room, to find out if the
snake lady and Mrs. P. was there. If they was, I was
thinking as how you and me, Emily, could make a little
trip to the end o' the tunnel to find out how them two
vanished last night.

"Well, the two o' them was there, all right, but
what was likewise there was a lot o' arguing and fighting
such as you ain't ever seen, with the snake lady screeching and hissing, and Mrs. P. hollering and snarling.
Next thing you know, 'fore I had a chance to break
'way, out from the room comes Cap'n Scurlock, bleed-
ing like a harpooned whale, as Pa always says.

" 'Let him go back to his ship and die!' screeches
the snake lady.

" 'We'll throw his body to the sharks later,' snarls
Mrs. P. sweetly.

"Meanwhilst, the Cap'n goes on staggering to the
stairs, and not wanting to be unfriendly like, I jump
from my hiding place, and offer him a hand. Nobody
notices us staggering out, which ain't surprising, things
running as they usually run at The Jolly Sailor. But
once we get outside, the Cap'n turns to me and says,
half-dead like, 'Ain't ee the boy what works from time
to time up at Sugar Hill Hall?'

" 'Same boy, though I don't work as much there
any more,' says I.

" 'But ee must know the child, Emily Luccock,' says he.

" 'That I do,' says I.

" 'Well, I must speak to her,' says he. 'There are things that I must tell her. I cannot go to my Maker with such dark secrets on my soul. So I'd be much obliged if ee would take me to Emily Luccock quick as ee can, because I ain't good for too many more breaths on this earth.'

" 'I'll do my bestest, Cap'n,' says I.

"But knowing as how with the size o' him and the size o' me, I might never make it to Sugar Hill Hall, why I brung him here to Pa's place. Pa and me decided as how I got to fetch you here, me promising the Cap'n on my life not to tell you 'bout who was requesting your presence. You know 'bout the rest, Emily. More tea?" Kipper hopped up and started for the kettle. Halfway there, he stopped and turned to the stairs, listening. "Sounds like Pa's back, and sounds like he's got someone with him!"

SEVENTEEN

A Stranger
at Pa's Place

From the small, dark opening into Kipper and Pa's quarters, there rose first a head of hair bright as a basket of oranges, followed by a face with cheeks whipped to a cheerful red by wind and sun, and a pair of sea-blue eyes that matched only one other pair in the world. This, then, had to be Kipper's Pa.

Directly behind him appeared another man in the uniform of a common seaman. Whatever portions of his face were not covered by a golden beard were deeply bronzed by the sun. His shoulders, broad as a hatch cover, seemed to fill the small room. And he was tall enough that he stooped when he reached the final step, as if from long experience he expected the top of his head to have an encounter with the ceiling.

Emily could not remember seeing this man in the cellar of The Jolly Sailor, but then there were so many around that ugly table. Perhaps he had been there. Kipper stared curiously, but when he started to speak, Pa motioned to him to be silent by putting a restraining finger to the lips. Then Pa motioned the stranger toward an unlit corner of the room. Without uttering a word, he went there and stood with his hands folded, staring silently across the room at the Captain.

"Now, who have we here?" Kipper's Pa's voice was as cheerful as a sunny day at the shore. He beamed at Emily as if there were no hint of a drama having to do with life and death being enacted in his home.

"This here's Emily, Pa," Kipper said. "And Emily, this here's Pa."

"Ain't ever been happier to meet anyone in my life!" said Pa. " 'Course I can't deny I would o' preferred livelier circumstances."

"I'm very pleased to meet you too!" Emily said, and dropped him a curtsy. "Mr.—" She stopped shyly for want of a proper name to use.

"Well now," said Pa, "since you ain't got one o' your own, and since all Kipper's friends do likewise, why I'd be pleased as the tuna what found a hole in the net, as I always say, to have you call me Pa."

"Thank you, Pa," said Emily.

Pa smiled broadly, but a moment later the smile had faded into a deep frown as he motioned toward the grim object lying across the room. "Has he spoke any words yet, Kipper?"

"Ain't said anything, Pa."

But as if he had heard them, Captain Scurlock gave a terrible groan. "Water! Water!"

"Fetch him a cup, Kipper," Pa said.

When Kipper returned with the water, Pa thrust a folded blanket under the Captain's head, and Kipper held the cup to his lips.

"Thankee!" the Captain whispered hoarsely. Then after several deep, painful breaths, he said, "Be she here—the child, Emily Luccock?"

"Right here, Cap'n," said Kipper. He motioned to Emily to draw nearer the bunk so the Captain might see her.

Emily gathered every ounce of courage she had to cross the room again, this time under the piercing gaze of the stranger standing motionless as a tombstone in the dark corner.

With great difficulty, the Captain turned his head to stare at her hard and long. "Aye, she be the one. And—and the other, fishmonger, be he here, too?"

"Here too, Cap'n," replied Pa, but he made no move to invite the stranger to the bunk.

"Good! Good! And did ee bring the papers, son?"

"Here, Cap'n." Kipper thrust the sheaf of papers into Captain Scurlock's outstretched hand.

"Thankee! Thankee! Now, give me a moment to rest before I speak again." The Captain's eyes drifted shut, and for several moments he lay so still it seemed that he had died. But at length his eyes opened once more. With trembling hands he lifted the papers and read wordlessly.

"These be the ones, all right. These be the papers from the lawyer firm of Dowling, Dowling, and Fairwell, stating that Emily Luccock's pa died a rich man. And Emily's ma being also dead, all the money being stolen by Plumly and Meeching, Inc. belongs rightfully to the child, Emily. Here!" Captain Scurlock lay his head back with a groan. "Read 'em!"

Kipper took the papers from his hands and parcelled them out to Emily and Pa. After that, the room was silent as they read, except for an occasional *"Wheeoo!"* from Kipper or Pa. Finally, Kipper looked at Emily. His eyes were huge.

"Dingus, Emily, you're a hairess!"

"Ain't any question 'bout that," said Pa.

"But—but I don't understand," stammered Emily. "Why did Aunt Twice tell me Papa died a pauper?"

"Is the Aunt Twice ee speaks of the same as Mrs. William Dorcas Luccock?" the Captain asked weakly.

Emily nodded.

"Well, child, the reason for that is because she received a letter as to that fact."

"A—a letter?"

"Forgery!" gasped Captain Scurlock. "All letters received by her—forgeries. All letters *sent* by her, likewise, after being stolen by the earlier mentioned Plumly and Meeching, Inc."

Emily looked with questioning eyes at Pa and Kipper and turned back to Captain Scurlock. "Why—why are you telling me all these things now?"

"Because I ain't got long to live, child, and I don't want more murders on my soul!" groaned the Captain.

"Murders!" Pa blurted out. "In what way murders, Cap'n?"

"So happens, fishmonger, if anything goes amiss with the child, Emily, then all falls to her Aunt Twice. Plumly and Meeching, Inc., courtesy of another forgery, are seeing to it that if anything goes amiss with the child's Aunt Twice, all falls to *them*. Ee can pretty well figure out the rest!"

Emily and Aunt Twice to be murdered! Certainly there was no question now that Emily must run away, and with Aunt Twice, if possible.

"But—but what about the old people?" Emily asked. "What is to happen to them?"

"The old people are a sad cover for a very ugly book, child. But far as I know, nought worse will happen to them than has already happened. It was only the above-mentioned murders that caused the fight that did me in. Smuggling and stealing all that loot was one thing, but murder o' Emily Luccock and her aunt I wanted nought to do with. My first mate Sneed, he wasn't so particular, so he sided up with Plumly and Meeching, Inc., and I got the business end o' his knife in my chest!" Moaning with pain, the Captain paused. "Now, for the benefit o' some in this room, what I say next had best be put in writing. So if someone will take up pen and a piece o' paper, writing while I speak, I'd be much obliged."

Kipper ran to the chest at once for pen, ink, and paper, as Pa said, "Kipper, our handwriting ain't such as most folks can rightly read it. Mayhap Emily best take pen in hand for the Cap'n."

So it was Emily who knelt down on the floor beside the dying Captain, and by the trembling light of the small brass lantern on the bedpost put down the words that he spoke.

"I, Captain Zacheus Zachariah Scurlock, being o' sound mind, if not sound body, do hereby confess that Seaman William Dorcas Luccock, o' the ship *Silver Sea,* never did commit the murder o' one Bellamy Q. Biggs, o' the same ship, five years past after a gambling quarrel, but instead was drugged and had placed in his hand one o' the bloody knives used to kill the same by Prunella Blossom Plumly, Theodosia Sly Meeching and I, the above-mentioned Captain Scurlock. Whether mine was the one o' the three knives that finished Bellamy Q. Biggs, I know not, but I cannot go to my maker with it upon my conscience, and I cannot go likewise without proclaiming the innocence o' William Dorcas Luccock.

"These long years have Plumly, Meeching, *and* Scurlock, Inc. held the threat of the hangman's noose over his head, keeping his wife in fear and terror for his life, and taking over the great mansion of Sugar Hill Hall, which by rights belongs to him, though he lost all else by gambling and a wild life, long since regretted." The Captain took a deep, agonizing breath, gathering strength to continue. "Now quickly, child, for my life is fast fading, give me the pen and paper and let me put my name to it."

With shaking fingers, Emily placed the pen in the gnarled hand, and the paper under it.

Uncle Twice *really* alive! Uncle Twice the one all along whom Aunt Twice had been protecting! Uncle Twice, whose very life had hung on her being a prisoner of the dread Mrs. Plumly and Mrs. Meeching! And Uncle Twice now freed of all blame for a crime he never did commit!

"Uncle Twice alive and well!" breathed Emily.

"Aye, child, alive and well and in this very room! Now go ee and take him this confession, signed before witnesses!"

Uncle Twice in that room? Where? The bronzed, bearded, broad-shouldered stranger looked nothing at all like the pale, slender man pictured in Emily's locket. She looked around the room in confusion.

Then the man stepped out of the shadows and stood in full light with his arms outstretched, and it *was* Uncle Twice! Tears streaming down her cheeks, Emily ran into the waiting arms and felt them fold around her. At long, long last, she was home!

"My darling Emily, forgive me for remaining silent, but I came to this room a murderer, and I thought I might leave a murderer. And never did I want you to know me as that! It was only by this confession that I could make myself known to you."

No sooner had Uncle Twice said these words, than the Captain raised his hand weakly, wanting to be heard. "I have no right to ask forgiveness of ee, William Luccock, but I ask it all the same, if ee can find it in thy heart to forgive."

With Emily's hand in his, Uncle Twice drew close to the Captain. "Because of what was done to my wife and this innocent child, I find it hard to forgive now. Perhaps in time I will be able to. But for myself, I *do* forgive, and for saving the lives of these so precious to me, I do also thank you with all my heart!"

"I thankee!" said the Captain. " 'Tis more than I deserve."

By now his face had become such a ghastly color and his breathing so difficult for him, it was clear his life was rapidly ebbing away. Tears again poured down Emily's face, this time for the old man, now losing his life for having tried to save hers.

"Shed no tears for me, Emily Luccock," he said,

"for I'm as blackhearted a villain as ever lived."

"No, never!" sobbed Emily, and she bent over and placed a kiss on the terrible scar that stabbed across his face.

"Thankee, child!" he whispered. Then his head rolled over, and he died.

Pa removed the blanket from under his head and gently laid it over his grizzled face. For moments, there was silence in the small room as thcy all gazed in sadness at the dead Captain.

Then Pa turned to Uncle Twice. "What's to be done now, sir?"

"What do *you* think best, sir?" replied Uncle Twice, returning the compliment by addressing Kipper's Pa as *sir*. For it was easy to see that in his eyes, the fishmonger was every bit as much a gentleman as he himself had been and was to be again.

"I think as how we ain't got a choice but to pay a visit to the police for you to present your credentuals, followed by a visit to The Jolly Sailor to present Mrs. Plumly and Mrs. Meeching with *their* comeuppance. You and me can take care o' that, whilst Kipper and Emily fly back to Sugar Hill Hall to carry the happy news to her Aunt Twice." Pa beamed at the two children before him.

"How 'bout Little Shrimper, Pa?" Kipper asked. "He ain't needed to keep watch now."

"Well, looks as how first thing I got to do is pay a visit to his ma and make a delivery that ain't got anything to do with fish, Kipper!"

Pa leaned over and scooped Little Shrimper up in his strong arms. Despite all the drama being enacted in the little boy's presence that night, he had been unable to hold up any longer. With his head dropped on the table, he had once again fallen fast asleep.

EIGHTEEN

Peppermints in the Parlor

It wasn't until she was racing along beside Kipper through the dark streets with Pa's splendid warm fishy coat flapping comfortingly about her knees, that an alarming thought struck Emily. *"The tunnel!"* she gasped.

"What 'bout the tunnel?" Kipper asked.

"Well, if Mrs. Plumly and Mrs. Meeching should learn about Uncle Twice and Pa coming for them with the policemen, wouldn't they try to escape?" said Emily. She was panting breathlessly as she scurried to keep up with Kipper.

"If I was in them shoes, *I* would," Kipper replied. "But what's it got to do with the tunnel?"

"Mightn't they try to escape through *it?*" said Emily. "Then they could collect some of the jewels in the ballroom on their way."

"Dingus, Emily, you're right!" Kipper exclaimed. "Knowing them two, that's exactly what they'd be likely to do. Pa don't know 'bout that tunnel either, 'cause I never told him for fear he'd have ten fish fits, as he always says, 'bout my messing 'round with such a nasty business. But then"—Kipper paused to think—"your Uncle Twice probably knows 'bout it, 'cause Sugar Hill Hall belongs to him."

"No, Kipper, he *doesn't!*" Emily said anxiously. "Don't you remember my telling you about the well he never had opened?"

Kipper frowned. "But there's them other steps and trapdoor too, Emily. I mean, the ones into the ballroom."

"The steps are much, much newer than the ones to the Remembrance Room," Emily said. "I noticed it when we went up them. And even though I was only a very small girl when I was first at Sugar Hill Hall, I remember Uncle Twice waltzing me right over the very place where the trapdoor is now. I think Mrs. Plumly and Mrs. Meeching must have had the steps and trap-door made, and Uncle Twice knows nothing about it."

"Which explains a lot o' things," said Kipper. "Them two lovely ladies must o' found out 'bout the tunnel private like and wanted to get their hands on it. They could o' just done in your Uncle Twice, but then they would o' had to finish off your Aunt Twice, and after that your ma and pa and you, who would doubt-less o' got Sugar Hill Hall, being next o' kin. But *all* those murders *all* together might o' raised a couple o' eyebrows. So they made special 'rangements to get your Uncle Twice out o' the way, and to get Sugar Hill Hall and the free services o' your Aunt Twice as well. *Wheeoo!*" Kipper whistled at having finally discovered the roots of all the dark and evil events.

"Well, if Uncle Twice and Pa don't know about the tunnel, and the ladies come through it, *we're* the ones who will have to stop them!" cried Emily.

"Just *us?*" said Kipper.

"There's Aunt Twice and Tilly and all the old people as well," Emily said.

Kipper scratched an ear doubtfully. "Your Aunt Twice and Tilly might do, but don't know as how we can count on them timid old ones."

"Timid old ones!" cried Emily, outraged. "How can you call someone timid who dared to take two peppermints and go to the Remembrance Room? And think of them all taking care of Clarabelle practically under Mrs. Meeching's very nose, and—and—" Emily was too furious to go on.

Kipper hunched his shoulders and grinned. "Ouch, Emily! I shouldn't o' said that. Agreed that the old ones can help, too. But what can all us brave people use to stop them two vipers—bare hands?"

"No!" Emily shook her head. "I've thought of something, something I saw that time I ran into Mrs. Meeching's room to rescue Mr. Bottle's peppermint." She looked furtively over her shoulder, because even now it still seemed that the eyes and ears of Sugar Hill Hall were everywhere. Then she whispered something to Kipper.

Kipper looked at her with sparkling eyes. "Dingus, Emily!" he exclaimed. "If you ain't the one!"

§❧

As soon as they entered Sugar Hill Hall, Kipper vanished up the stairs, and Emily was left with the joyful task of waking Aunt Twice with the most wonderful news in the whole world. There was, however, one disheartening problem that remained. Uncle Twice, after all his rugged years at sea, had become suntanned, husky, and handsomer than ever, while Aunt Twice, with all her worries and fears, had become thin, wan, and weary. Could Uncle Twice still love her? Emily wondered. Would he?

Fortunately, she had little time to ponder this question, because she was too busy with the difficult task of waking a Tilly who could have stayed asleep if the entire mansion had come crashing down about her ears. Then Emily had to reveal all the news about Mrs. Plumly, the tunnel and the tavern, and of course, Uncle Twice.

"Well, I ain't never!" cried Tilly. The look of surprise and shock in her watery blue eyes gave promise of staying there forever. But after Emily had told her everything, it was the simplest matter to enlist her aid in helping put an end to the two tyrants who had ruled over her for such a large portion of her life.

Then Aunt Twice, Tilly, and Emily all sped to the parlor where Kipper, like the Pied Piper, was just leading Mrs. Poovey, Mrs. Loops, Mr. Bottle, Mr. Dobbs, Mrs. Quirk and all the other old people down the broad staircase. They were still in their shabby flannel bathrobes and rundown slippers, rubbing the sleep from their eyes, but they had an air of excitement about them despite having just been awakened and given a quick history of the recent dramatic events.

"Emily, you dear, darling child!" cried Mrs. Poovey and Mrs. Loops in unison. They rushed to Emily and threw their arms around her.

"Oh Emily, you're safe and well, you absolutely are!" said Mr. Bottle, blowing his nose from sheer joy.

Mrs. Quirk dashed away a happy tear. "We were

afraid we'd never see you again, dear child."

It was some time before Emily could even catch her breath from all the violent hugging and squeezing. "Do you know all that's happened?" she asked. "Did Kipper tell you?"

Mrs. Poovey bobbed her head. "Oh yes, dear, he did. He came to tell Mrs. Loops and me first."

"And *we* helped him tell all the others," added Mrs. Loops, quivering proudly under her enormous lavender flannel bathrobe.

"I hope you're not too frightened," Emily said.

"Well, as a matter of fact we *are*, dear," said Mrs. Poovey. "But, oh my, even if it meant spending the rest of our days in the Remembrance Room, we wouldn't want to miss this, would we, Mrs. Loops?"

"Certainly not!" replied Mrs. Loops, beaming.

"Nor would any of us!" said Mr. Bottle wetly but happily, from behind his handkerchief.

"Now, here's Kipper handing out our weapons!" said Mr. Dobbs. His old face, as wrinkled as parchment, was aglow with excitement.

They all waited with breathless anticipation as Kipper handed out paper bags retrieved from the kitchen. Tilly quickly peeked into her bag, and then raised happy, disbelieving eyes.

"Well, I declares!" she exclaimed.

The gaslights were turned down whisper low, and a conspiratorial hush fell on the parlor as they all stood in the shadows, silently observed only by the dust, the cobwebs and the plaster cupids overhead.

They did not have long to wait. What Emily had thought might happen was exactly what did happen. Through the thick walls of the old ballroom were wafted the muffled screeches and hisses, snarls and screams of two ladies having a polite argument.

"It's all your fault!" howled one.

"Ha! Ha! and *ha! My* fault, indeed!" yelled the other.

"Snake!"

"Viper!"

"Fool!"

"Jackass!"

Moments after this exchange of pleasantries, the door from Mrs. Meeching's room flew open, and out burst Plumly and Meeching, Inc., coats thrown on any which way, and hair flying about like haystacks in a windstorm. Each one carried two enormous black carpetbags spilling over with jewels greedily snatched up in the ballroom. But they were brought to a sudden, dramatic stop when their furious eyes fell on Emily, Kipper, Aunt Twice, Tilly, and all the old people lined up solidly as a stone wall before the front door.

"Aaaaaaaargh!" snarled Mrs. Plumly.

"Sssssssssss!" hissed Mrs. Meeching.

"Step aside at once!" commanded Mrs. Plumly. Then she collected herself enough to add slyly, "You will all be rewarded with peppermints." When she saw that this had no effect, however, she screamed, "If you don't, you'll all go back to moldy bread!"

"And the Remembrance Room!" screamed Mrs. Meeching.

As there was still no sign of anyone even hearing them, much less minding, Mrs. Plumly drew her two evil knitting needles from a carpetbag. "Move away, if you don't want to feel the points of these!"

But even as she was spitting out the words, the hands of Aunt Twice and Tilly, Kipper and Emily, Mrs. Poovey and Mrs. Loops and all the other old people were dipping into the bags Kipper had given them.

"Are you ready, Mrs. Loops?" Mrs. Poovey was heard to say.

"Quite ready, Mrs. Poovey," replied Mrs. Loops.

"Then heave ho, and aim!" cried Mrs. Poovey.

And then all at once, a storm of puffy, tempting, tantalizing, delicious, pink-and-white-striped peppermint drops, become stinging hailstones in the hands of the outraged residents of Sugar Hill Hall, burst through the parlor at Mrs. Plumly and Mrs. Meeching.

"Fiends!" screeched Mrs. Meeching.

"Vultures!" screamed Mrs. Plumly.

Faces contorted with hatred and fury, the two ladies were driven back across the parlor by the hailstorm of stinging peppermints.

"Quick, the kitchen!" hissed Mrs. Meeching. But

by the time they had headed for that escape route, it was too late. From behind them, as well as through the front door, were already pouring a dozen policemen with chains, nets, and clubs. It was but a matter of a few moments for Plumly and Meeching, Inc. to be chained up, locked, and removed from Sugar Hill Hall forever.

Still, with all of that, Emily did not feel entirely satisfied until Uncle Twice finally stepped through the door with Kipper's Pa. But when she saw the look on Uncle Twice's face as his eyes found Aunt Twice, and saw her run into his arms laughing and crying at the same time, then Emily was truly happy at last. For it was clear that Uncle Twice found Aunt Twice to be more beautiful than ever!

So everything was now solved, and everything settled. Sugar Hill Hall was returned to its rightful owners. Uncle and Aunt Twice would live there with Emily, whose great wealth would help keep them until Uncle Twice should regain his own fortune. And Emily's dear friends, Mrs. Poovey, Mrs. Loops, Mr. Bottle, Mr. Dobbs, Mrs. Quirk and all the other old people would live there too, enjoying warm, cozy rooms, splendid meals, and the joy of playing with Clarabelle to their heart's content.

With so much happiness, why should anyone weep? And yet, standing forlornly in one corner of the parlor was Tilly, her pale eyes flooded with tears. Emily ran to her at once.

"Tilly, what's the matter? Why are you crying when everything is all happiness now?"

"It ain't all happiness for me!" sobbed Tilly. "Us orphings was getting to be good friends. Now y'r a hairess, Emily, and you ain't going to wants me 'round no more."

"What a foolish thing to say!" exclaimed Emily. "Why not?"

" 'Cause—'cause I ain't been as good a friend as I oughts when you was poor, pinching you and all that 'cause I was greener than any pea with envy on 'count o' you havings y'r Aunt Twice, and me not havings nobody. But worse than that, I *stoled* from you, Emily!"

"Stole from me?" said Emily. "What did you steal, Tilly?"

"This!" said Tilly miserably. From the pocket of her dress she pulled Emily's bedraggled white fur tam-o'-shanter. It was worn almost to the skin from having been rubbed to death.

"Why, Tilly," said Emily promptly, "you didn't steal that from me. You only *borrowed* it, don't you remember?"

"I *dids?*" said the amazed Tilly.

"Yes, and I'm certain as can be that one day you were going to return it to me," said Emily firmly.

"I *were?*" said the astonished Tilly, beaming. "You means we can go on being friends, Emily?"

"Of course!" declared Emily. "And you shall not only have your very own fur tam-o'-shanter now, Tilly, but all the pretty things you want. And you shall move upstairs from the cellar to live next to me, and we shall have lessons together, and—"

"Lessons?" said Tilly faintly. She looked like a bird whose owner has just set it free only to turn around and put an arrow through its heart.

"Well, you don't have to if you don't want to," said Emily quickly. "But if you do, you may, and we shall always remain the best of friends!"

After this happily received speech, Emily ran back to Aunt and Uncle Twice, to be hugged again by one and swung, laughing, into the air by the other. Then she skipped over to Kipper, who was standing nearby with Pa. Both faces were alight with cheerful grins.

"Just think, Kipper!" she cried. "Never again will there be shadows in Sugar Hill Hall, just sunshine and peppermints in the parlor for everyone, forever!"

After long moments of silence, in which neither Kipper nor Pa could think of anything grand enough to say to this joyful pronouncement, Kipper finally came up with a speech.

"Dingus, Emily!"

"As Kipper always says," concluded Pa happily.